HER LAST HOUR

DANIEL HURST

www.danielhurstbooks.com

Download My Free Book

*If you would like to receive a FREE copy of my
psychological thriller 'Just One Second', then you can
find the link to the book at my website
www.danielhurstbooks.com*

1

Time is precious. Time is money. And time is the only thing we can't beat.

But tonight, I'm not going to worry about what the hands on the clock say. I won't be a slave to time, trying to rush and get things done at a hundred miles per hour like I usually do.

Tonight, I'm going to break the habit of a lifetime and do something I probably should have done a while ago.

I'm going to waste time.

Even the thought of it is enough to make me nervous but that's precisely why I need to do it. I've worked far too hard for far too long, and while I'm not planning on retiring and putting my feet up permanently yet, I have more than earnt the right to take things easy for one night.

It's Friday, which makes this the perfect point in the week for a little relaxation, and as I glance at the clock and see that it's just after eight in the evening, I vow to make that the last occasion in which I consult the time today.

Having just spent ten minutes in the shower washing my hair and cleansing my body of all the dust, dirt, and God knows what else it might have picked up while I was in London earlier, I now need to get dressed but before I do, I think about checking my emails on my phone. Fortunately, I catch myself just before I open my inbox, reminding myself that I just vowed to have the night off.

Old habits die hard, I suppose, but I resist the temptation to check anything work-related. But the same can't be said for things associated with my personal life, and I make a quick check on my messages to see if there is anything new there. More specifically, I'm looking to see if my brother has replied to the text I sent him earlier today, the one in which I said I hoped he was doing well and was thinking of him, as always.

But, also as always, he has not replied to me, which makes that over fifty messages I've sent him in this past year without getting a response.

But who's counting?

Returning to my plan of having a phone-free Friday night, I hold down the power button on my device until the light on the screen cuts out, and with my mobile out of action, I place it in my bedside drawer and make a point of forgetting about it until the morning.

I make my way to my wardrobe next, my bare feet padding across my plush bedroom carpet, the one that only got laid a couple of weeks ago and took three men to fit, although they were putting new carpet throughout the entire house, so it was a big job.

I made sure to make them plenty of cups of tea throughout their stay, though, as well as give them a healthy chunk of cash by way of a tip at the end to thank them for all their hard work. They were very appreciative, as well as slightly apologetic for some of the colourful language they had used as they were toiling away, but the main thing was that they had done a good job and made this house look much more presentable.

And it certainly needed a facelift.

I only moved into this property a month ago, and like all house moves, it's been a hectic time. But I've tried not to let the stress of all that take away from the fact that this really is my dream home.

It's a two-storey new build, very modern and was only built a decade ago by a German designer called Franz, who made this his passion project.

Having purchased a sizeable patch of land in the Kent countryside, Franz set about building his ideal home, and from what the estate agent told me, he was involved in every step of the process, from the architect's blueprints to overseeing the construction workers who dug the foundations and slowly but surely erected this magnificent structure.

Franz and his family moved in as soon as the project was completed and, from what I'm told, spent many happy years here, right up until the point when Franz's wife got ill and wished to move back to their homeland.

The German was a very reluctant seller considering how much time and affection he had put into the building of this place, but he eventually opted to put the house up for sale for the sake of his wife's wish to move home, and when he did, I was the fortunate beneficiary of that.

Well, after I'd forked out over one million pounds for it, so it didn't exactly fall into my lap.

I fell in love with this place as soon as I saw it, and while there were plenty of other offers from eager buyers, I was the only one who could pay the full asking price upfront, so Franz accepted the quick sale and then went back to Germany with his family to care for his sick wife. But I could see how much love and attention he had put into this place, and after feeling bad for the reasons why he ultimately had to sell, I made sure to give a sizeable donation to a charity associated with the disease that was threatening his partner.

I wish I could have done more for them, but sadly, there are some things money can't buy and health is one of them.

Having been handed the keys by the estate agent, a man who hadn't stopped grinning from ear to ear due to the juicy commission he had earnt himself brokering this deal, I entered this house with my mind full of exciting possibilities.

A new colour scheme in the kitchen. Converting one of the spare bedrooms into an office. A little landscaping in the garden. There was a lot that I wanted to do, and once I was the proud owner, I had all the time in the world to do it. But redecorating is a slow process, and while I'm making steady headway, there's still a long way to go.

Some of the rooms are still full of boxes that I haven't unpacked yet, and I'm constantly forgetting where I put things, opening cupboards and drawers only to remember that what I'm looking for is somewhere else. But I'll get there and when I do, I'll really have a home to be proud of.

But just like I plan to forget about my day job this evening, so too do I plan on pushing all thoughts of redecorating from my mind.

I quickly dry my hair, my dark locks flowing out at the sides of me as the hairdryer does its job before I apply a little moisturiser, trying not to pay too much attention to my tired appearance in the mirror because it's been a long week, so I'll just put it down to the early mornings and late nights rather than me edging another few days closer to my 39th birthday.

After slipping into a comfy pair of pyjamas and wrapping myself in my fluffy dressing gown, I'm ready to go downstairs and make myself some dinner.

I am looking forward to making a small portion of vegetable risotto, a healthy meal that I was used to making all the time before I became extremely busy at work and found myself scoffing takeaways and putting on a little excess weight as I put my career before my waistline. But a new start in this house is my motivation to clean up my diet, and while I might wash down my meal with a glass of white wine tonight, the food I put into my mouth will be of the healthy variety.

Reaching the top of my large spiral staircase, I briefly glance at all the bare walls and consider the artwork I want to display here one day, artwork that is still in storage in London but will soon be making its way to me when I have the time to arrange it. But that's yet another job for another day, and I go downstairs before I become too overwhelmed with my sizeable To-Do list.

My stomach rumbles slightly as my feet move off the carpet steps and pass onto the marble tiles that cover the floor in the hallway, and I have to be a little careful not to slip in my socks on this slick surface.

That's one thing about marble that Franz possibly didn't consider when he was building this place. It might look good and add a touch of class, but it's very slippery, and I imagine it's like an ice rink when it's wet after being mopped. But again, that's a problem for another day because tonight is all about switching off from the nagging necessities of life.

With my back to the front door, I'm just about to enter the kitchen when I hear the fluttering of the letterbox behind me.

Turning around, my first thought is that the wind has caught it because I doubt there are any postmen out delivering letters to people at this time of night, especially not my postman, who seems to come and go when he can be bothered rather than when I actually have some mail to receive. But I'm wrong because I see a white envelope slide through the slit in the door before falling to the tile below, and it makes a soft landing before the letterbox closes and whoever just posted it through has gone.

I walk over to the envelope and scoop it up, eager to look inside it because if it isn't for me and the person outside has got the wrong house, then I'd rather catch them before they've left; otherwise, I'll have to make a trip to the post box to have it redirected to the correct recipient. But then I see that this envelope is definitely for me, and I know that because it has my name written in black ink across the front of it.

Katherine.

Opening the envelope, I pull out the white piece of paper held inside it and open it up.

When I do, I see one short sentence written in more black ink across the middle of the page. But no sooner have I read it than the paper falls from my hand and lands by my feet at the foot of the door.

It's shocking.

It's terrifying.

I can scarcely believe what I'm reading.

It says I have one hour to live.

2

My first thought after reading the letter is that it's a prank. Somebody is playing a joke on me.

And that somebody must still be outside my house now.

If I'm quick, then I could catch them, and before I know it, I'm reaching for the key that's poking out of the lock in my door, knowing a simple twist of it will allow me to open the door and hopefully catch the sender on my doorstep before they can run away. But I pause at the last second because suddenly, opening the door doesn't feel like the most sensible thing to do.

What if this isn't a joke?

What if the person who wrote this letter is serious?

What if they really want to kill me?

The door remains closed and, more importantly, locked as I quickly consider my options.

Either I believe what this letter says or I don't.

If I don't, then my chance to catch whoever has played this sick game is fading by the second because they'll most likely be running away now, and it won't be long until they're off down the street, getting away scot-free. I have a gate at the top of my driveway but I'm guessing they just climbed over that, which is worrying in itself.

But if I do take this seriously, and surely I can't risk not doing so, then I can't open this door and them climbing over the gate suggests they really were eager to deliver it to me.

If this is real, I have to stay in here.

Where it's safe.

Letting go of the key, I look down at the letter at my feet. But before I pick it up, I realise I don't have to go outside to potentially see who posted it.

Running into my living room, I reach for the curtains and pull them open, allowing me to peer out through my window onto my dark driveway. As I do, I can see the silhouette of my car parked out there, exactly where I left it when I got back home half an hour ago. I can also see the tall hedges that line the sides of my front garden, screening my property from the neighbours, although now I kind of wish they could see me and I could see them because it might make me feel a little safer. But I can see something else too.

Footprints.

We had a sprinkling of snow earlier, a mid-winter flurry that coated this town in white and was pretty to look out on but tricky to drive in on the roads. But that snow allows me to detect if anybody has come to my door other than me and sure enough, I see two sets of footprints out there.

Mine.

And somebody else's.

The bigger footprints come from the gate and lead to my door before seeming to return to the gate, making me more confident that whoever did this has gone back the way they came. At least they're not lurking down the side of the house, and that's something to be grateful for, I suppose.

They must have already run away, and a big part of me rues the fact that I don't have a security camera installed over my front door recording all the comings and goings at my property. Unfortunately, a camera installation is just one of the many things on my To-Do list, and I hadn't got around to having an engineer come out and do that yet, though it is necessary because homes like mine are prime targets for burglars. But whoever has just been here has taken advantage of my delay in securing this place a little more efficiently and because of that, I have no way of catching them.

Unless they come back...

With nothing going on outside my house, my thoughts return to the letter, and I go back into the hallway to pick it up. My hands are shaking slightly as I reread it, but I'm not sure if that's because I'm scared or because I'm angry. I guess that all depends on if I believe what's written on this piece of paper.

You have one hour to live.

That's it. That's the message. Six words. No context. No explanation. No further sentence for me to understand this any better. Just one simple statement, clearly designed to send a shiver down my spine.

Well, it's worked, and to prove it, I glance up at the clock on the wall of the hallway to see what the time is. But I'm not just curious about what point of the evening I am at now. Rather, I'm making a mental note so I know exactly what time it is when my hour begins.

That way, I'll know when it will be due to expire.

But thinking that way only serves the purpose of making me even more afraid, as well as making me feel a little foolish, so I refocus and try to figure this out.

Why would somebody say this to me?

Why try and frighten a woman living by herself?

And why would anybody want me dead?

I wish I could just ignore this letter. Screw it up and toss it in the bin. Pretend like it never happened. Go back to what I was planning on doing, which was cooking a nice meal and having a drink.

But how can I?

I have to take this seriously because maybe it is and if that's the case, then there's only one thing I can do.

I have to call the police.

After double-checking again that the door is still locked, I take the letter and head back upstairs, feeling a little safer as I go at putting some more distance between me and whoever might still be lurking out there on the perimeter of my home. They can come to my door, but they can't climb a wall, or at least I doubt they can unless they're some kind of agile cat burglar, so they won't be able to trouble me now that I'm up on a higher floor.

Once I'm in my bedroom, then I rush over to the bedside table, the one that currently has a copy of my latest read sitting on top of it. It's a self-help book titled *60 Seconds To A Stress-free Life,* but funnily enough, this isn't quite the right time to be thumbing through the pages and reading about the author's theories that may or may not work in reality. Instead, I'm more interested in what's inside the bedside table, and as I open the drawer, I'm planning on taking out my mobile phone, turning it on and dialling 999 as quickly as possible.

But then I open the drawer and suddenly, the letter in my hand is not the scariest thing that has happened to me tonight.

That's because the drawer is empty.

My phone has gone.

3

'No,' I say out loud, almost trying to convince myself that what has just happened is impossible. My phone can't be missing. It has to be here. I only put it in this drawer a couple of moments ago.

I'd just had a shower. I was going to check my emails. But then I decided against it and turned my phone off before putting it in here, out of sight and out of mind.

So how can it be gone now?

I must have got the wrong drawer. That has to be it. I thought I'd put it in the top drawer, but I must be mistaken. It'll be in the second drawer.

Right?

Wrong. The second drawer is empty too, as is the third. My phone is definitely not in any part of my bedside table, despite the fact that I definitely left it here earlier. That can only mean that somebody has taken it out.

And that means somebody is in my house.

I feel my chest tighten and my breath catch in my throat as I consider the horrible possibility that somebody has broken into my home and is now only moments away from attacking me. It must be the person who posted the letter.

Who else could it be?

They were giving me a warning, and now they've come to take more decisive action. I don't know who they are or why they want to hurt me, but there's no time for questions.

They're inside.

And now I'm vulnerable.

I'm so afraid that I almost wish whoever was after me would just come in here and get it over with. Attack me. Kill me. Put me out of my misery. Anything has to be better than this torment of fear and uncertainty. But nothing has happened. Nobody has appeared with a knife or other such weapon.

I'm still alive.

For now, anyway.

The extra few seconds I seem to have been mercifully afforded gives me the opportunity to try and figure out how somebody could have got in my house. But the more I think about it, the less I see how it is possible. I've been out at work all day, but the alarm system was activated, the same alarm system that was already installed in this property by the previous owner and was included in the purchase price.

I knew that it would be a hassle to have somebody rip out the old system and put in a new one in so I just kept whatever was here, and it should have been more than adequate. But the alarm had not been activated, so nobody could have come in here while I was at work.

Unless they entered after I arrived home?

Now I'm running through my movements since I got back. I parked my car on the drive. Picked up my handbag, then left my vehicle. Took out my front door keys. I also took out my phone and disabled the house alarm on the app before I entered. But that would have only given any possible intruder mere seconds to get in, so I doubt they were that lucky. Then I locked the door behind me immediately. It's sensible to do so anyway, but as a woman living alone, I never take any chances.

Once inside, I didn't open any windows. It's January, and the weather is freezing, meaning the central heating system is still preferred over fresh air for now. An intruder could not have come through a window then, at least not unless they literally smashed the glass before entering. But I would have heard such a thing, wouldn't I?

I was in the shower.

I suddenly realise that the ten minutes I spent in the bathroom, washing my hair and soaking my skin with soapy suds, could have been the time frame in which somebody illegally entered my home.

I wouldn't have heard any windows smashing with the hot water rushing past my ears and certainly not because I was playing music on my phone as well. A stupid song that I didn't need to be listening to and only put on to perk my mood up after a stressful day. But with all that noise in the upstairs bathroom, who's to say somebody didn't break and enter downstairs?

I think about how I quickly got dressed after my shower and went down to make food, but my progress into the kitchen was halted when I heard the letterbox flutter. Maybe I would have seen a broken window in there if I hadn't been interrupted. But there are many other rooms downstairs, and any one of them could have been where somebody gained access.

After reading the letter, I went to look outside via the living room window so at least I know that wasn't how anybody got in. But it could have been while doing that that somebody slipped upstairs and took my phone from the dressing table drawer. There's no other explanation for it going missing other than somebody moving it.

And that somebody could now be lurking behind any one of the doors in this house.

A big part of me wants to stay as still and as silent as I can manage, as if pretending that I'm not here will somehow confuse the intruder and keep me safe. But that's silly, so I consider another course of action.

Communicating with them.

Should I call out and try and get a response?

Is that wise?

Maybe I could negotiate with them. Find out why they are here. See if they'd be willing to take money to leave me alone. Or at least find out whereabouts they are hiding so it's less of a shock when they finally show themselves.

That's it. I'm doing it.

I'm going to try and talk my way out of this.

Swallowing hard and clenching my fists together, I look towards the open bedroom door and prepare to speak.

'Who's there?' I ask, but my voice comes across as faint. Weak. Not good enough.

'I know you're here,' I say, louder this time, more assertive and assured, which is frankly ridiculous because I feel anything but.

It doesn't matter. There's no response.

'What do you want?' I ask now, praying the answer is something I can give them, like cash, and not something that can't be replaced, like my life. But still no other sound from my quiet home.

'You probably already know this, but I have money,' I say, not being boastful, just honest. 'If that's what this is about, then I can get you some. Just tell me how much you need, and I'll sort it out. Nobody has to get hurt.'

By nobody, I mean me. I seriously doubt whoever I am talking to is worried about themselves coming to any harm.

After trying that, the silence I get in return is deafening. If they are here for money, then they aren't letting me know it. Then I think about the letter again. They've already told me what they are here to do.

They're here to kill me, and they will do so in less than one hour.

'I read your message,' I call out, doing my best to keep any shakiness out of my voice. 'Why do you want to hurt me?'

Nothing.

'What have I done to you?'

Still nothing.

'WHO ARE YOU?'

I almost surprise myself with the volume of my voice, never mind whoever might be listening to me. But it seems to do the trick because I get an answer this time, although it doesn't come in the form of words.

It comes as the lights in the house go off.

The power has been cut.

And now I'm plunged into darkness.

4

My first instinct is to run into the en-suite bathroom just off my bedroom and lock myself in there so that whoever is in my house with me in the darkness can't get me. But I know I'll be trapped in there, too afraid to come out from behind the locked door, and the thought that my tormentor wants to kill me tells me that would be a bad move.

What if they set fire to the house while I'm locked in there? I wouldn't know until smoke started creeping under the door and by then, it might already be too late. I'd be trapped on the upper floor, and the fire could be blocking all my escape routes.

I shouldn't stay up here. I need to try and get downstairs and get out of the house now. And as frightening as it is, maybe the darkness can be my friend.

I can't see whoever is doing this to me.

But they won't be able to see me either.

I take off, running towards the bedroom door without giving it another second's thought, forcing my body into motion before fear paralyses me and I'm rendered useless. I'm half expecting somebody to grab me as I leave the room and try and wrestle me to the floor, but I'm hoping that the speed of my movements might allow me to evade them. I was a cross-country runner back in my school days, and while those ended over twenty years ago and I'm much closer to forty than I am to fifteen, I have managed to maintain some level of the high fitness I once possessed.

Running in the dark and using my memory of the layout of my new home to guide me while I'm unable to fully see, I am on the landing now and turning towards the staircase. I know it'll be dangerous to run down the steps at high speed, but it's surely more dangerous to stay up here and go slow.

With my legs moving as fast as the times I tried to win first place in the class competitions that used to take place every Thursday afternoon at Milford High School, I bound down the staircase, my heart thumping and my senses screaming at me to slow down before I fall and break my neck. I used to think running over muddy fields and dodging puddles down dirt tracks was hard enough, but try racing down a spiral staircase with only the faintest glimmer of moonlight coming through the skylight high above to guide the way.

But I've made it. I'm downstairs, and nobody has grabbed me yet.

Now all I need to do is get to the front door, turn that key, and I'll be out in the fresh air...

I suddenly lose sight of the moonlight filtering through the glass above the front door as I lose my footing and fall backwards.

Oh no, I slipped on this damn marble floor.

What was I thinking trying to run across it in socks?

And then I make impact.

With no time to try and cushion my fall with my hands, I make a hard landing on the tiles, and a loud cry escapes my lips as I feel pain in my left elbow. That and my left hip took the brunt of the fall, and while I'm lucky I didn't bang my head, because that could have been disastrous, I'm still far from unscathed.

But there's no time to feel sorry for myself because I need to get back to my feet and get moving again. I'm a sitting duck here and a lame one at that, and it might only be seconds until somebody follows me down these stairs, if they haven't done so already.

I peer back behind me for a second, but I can't see anybody there, and now I'm on the move again, my elbow throbbing and my hip aching terribly as I go. There'll be time for me to assess my injuries later because all I care about now is getting outside and running to my next-door neighbours' house, making plenty of noise as I go in the hope that they'll hear me coming before I reach them and call the police without wasting any more time.

I reach the door and stuff my feet into a pair of old trainers before scrabbling around for the key, gritting my teeth as the pain from my fall does its best to overpower me. But the key isn't in the lock where it should be. That's missing too, just like my phone. And without it, I can't open this door and get out of here.

'No,' I cry, the emotion of the last few minutes overwhelming me and causing me to lose control of myself. But that doesn't help me locate the key because it's definitely not in the lock, and despite pulling on the handle, I can't escape.

It feels like whoever is tormenting me is always one step ahead, and as long as that is the case, then I've got no chance of surviving this. But I'm not going to waste time trying this escape route if it's already futile, so I turn and run towards the kitchen and the rear of the house.

Entering the kitchen, I see the red digits on the display on the oven, four glowing numbers that tell me the time, not that I wish to see that because I know I'm already fighting against a ticking clock with every second that passes by.

I have more grip on my feet now, thanks to the trainers, so the tiles in here aren't as slippery as those in the hallway, but I still almost manage to slide into the breakfast bar in the centre of the kitchen through sheer momentum, only managing to stop myself before I do any more damage to my battered and bruised body. The breakfast bar was one of the many features I loved about this home when I viewed it, but now it's merely an obstacle between me and the back door and as I scurry around it, I'm wishing it wasn't so damn big.

I manage to get past it, although not before accidentally knocking the fruit bowl over that used to sit on top of it, and it crashes loudly on the floor as apples and oranges roll across the tiles and present even more hazards to me in this dark and dangerous setting.

My toes connect with an orange and send it into the bottom of one of the many cupboards in here, but I didn't trip, and now I'm at the back door. But I need the key, so I immediately turn to my left because I keep it inside a small tin just behind the bread bin.

Locating the tin in the dark is a challenge, one that's made even harder because I feel like I have to keep glancing back towards the hallway to see if anybody is coming in here behind me. But nobody is yet and once I find the tin, I think I'm finally starting to get the upper hand. I only feel even more confident when I open the tin and find the key inside because that's the first time in a while that something important is where it's supposed to be.

The tin falls to the floor and makes an almighty din, but I don't care about that as I do my best to stick the key in the lock, and despite a couple of miscues, I manage to slot it in.

Turning it emphatically, I pull on the handle, and the door opens, causing a huge wave of euphoria to rise up inside me as the cold outside air seeps into my home and hits me full in the face. I'm not exactly dressed for being outdoors in these temperatures, and my footwear isn't ideal, but at least I have my dressing gown to provide me with some warmth as I leave the house and run into my back garden.

'Help me!' I cry in the general direction of the house next door, although I'm still a distance away from them, and I doubt anybody there heard me unless they happened to be standing beside an open window, and that's unlikely. But I keep calling out as I run from the open kitchen door, making a quick route away from my property and planning on ducking through the hedges at the bottom of my garden.

I feel the water from the snow seeping into my trainers and soaking my socks as I move across the wet grass, but the moonlight is guiding the way, and I can see exactly where I need to go to get through. It's a small gap in the hedges that I noticed when I was out here last weekend, taking a closer look at my new back garden.

I'm not sure why one of the hedges had been removed by the previous owner to cause the slightly unsightly gap, but I figured it was nothing a good gardener couldn't sort out for me once the weather turned and spring was on the horizon. But it's that gap that will allow me to slip out of my garden and into next door's now, and as I keep my eyes on it, I feel like I am finally escaping this nightmare.

And then I see somebody step out of the shadows and block my way, forcing me to freeze before I run straight into them.

But whoever it is doesn't seem too worried about the prospect of me almost colliding with them because they stay very still, their eyes looking at me through the slits in the balaclava that is pulled over their head.

Maybe it's the fact that their identity is concealed that gives them such confidence.

Or maybe it's because they are holding a knife in their hand and pointing the blade right at me.

5

A small scream is all I can manage before a gloved hand goes over my mouth, and I'm prevented from making any more noise. I wrestle for a moment, but the cold edge of the blade that is pressed to my neck soon makes me realise that resisting is too dangerous.

I don't know who this person is, but the main thing is that they have a deadly weapon, so surviving is my priority, and I figure the best way to do that is to comply.

'Back inside the house. Now.'

My captor's instructions are simple, but he drags me towards the kitchen door that I just ran through as if he expects me to try and get away. I wish I could, but the grip he has on my left arm is firm, plus the knife is still only inches away from my windpipe, so there's very little I can do but go where he wants me to.

My trainers and socks are soaked in the slushy snow as we move back across the grass, but my captor has no such problems, thanks to the black boots on his feet. In the pale moonlight, I notice that the colour of his footwear matches the rest of his outfit.

Black combat trousers. A black hoody. And that black balaclava that continues to conceal his identity.

No wonder I didn't see him out here in the darkness until the last second.

'Get inside,' he says as he pushes me through the open door, and now I'm back in my kitchen again.

The door is closed and locked behind me, but in the split second that my captor's back is turned, I lunge for the drawer where I keep my cutlery in the hopes of pulling a knife of my own out to match his.

I manage to get the drawer open, and my hands scramble across various metallic utensils, but I'm unable to get a grip on anything useful before I'm pulled away from the drawer and admonished for what I just tried to do.

'Don't be so stupid. Do you want to die quicker than you have to?'

The question is a chilling one, making it clear that death is still coming for me, just not quite yet. But why prolong my misery?

Why are they dragging this out if they clearly want me dead?

'Who are you? What have I done to you?'

My desperate questions demand answers, and surely some honesty is the least I deserve, but I don't get any more information yet. Instead, my arm is gripped tightly again, and I'm marched out of the kitchen and into the hallway, the same place I slipped earlier and hurt myself, although the adrenaline coursing through my body seems to have taken the edge off that pain for the time being, not that I'm particularly grateful for that.

I wish my captor would slip now and give me another chance to get away, but there's little chance of that with the grip on his boots making it easier for him to maintain a steady footing. But I'm leaving a wet trail behind me on the floor, my soaking trainers squeaking as I move across the marble.

My captor's boots are loud on the hard surface beneath us, and I'm struck by the thought that it would have been almost impossible for him to move quickly over the marble earlier while I was in the house without his footsteps making too much noise and me hearing them. The fact I didn't hear anything makes me wonder how he could have managed it, but now we're in the dining room, and after being told to sit in one of the chairs at the table, my hands are pulled behind my back.

'What are you doing?' I ask, even though it's obvious the second I see the cable ties come out of the man's pockets.

My aggressor is quiet as he wraps the cable ties around my wrists and loops them through the back of the chair. Making a run for it just got a hell of a lot harder now that I'm attached to my seat.

My wrists are tugged and yanked as he inspects his work before he leaves me be, and I guess he's satisfied with the job he has done in restraining me. But I make sure to pull my arms and test his skills with the cable ties, although sadly for me, I only get confirmation that he has done a sufficient job, and I'm now tied up without hope of escape.

The man takes a step back and studies me for a moment, and I watch his eyes through the holes in his balaclava. They're deep blue, and I try to think if I have seen them anywhere before. But it's difficult to recognise somebody when you can only see a fraction of their features, so I'm still none the wiser.

I do notice that the hole in which the left eye is peering out of is slightly larger than the one on the right, though that is hardly a discernible detail that will help me identify the man wearing it.

'Who are you?' I ask again, only I'm a little calmer this time. I'm hoping that by behaving more rationally, I might get the same in return.

Without answering me, my captor reaches into his pocket and takes out a small digital device and I keep watching it closely as he types on it. Then I notice the man check his watch and once he has, he sets the device down in the middle of the table, far enough away from me to taunt me but not too far that I can't see what is on the screen.

There's a series of numbers, and they are counting down.

It's a timer, and it's showing me how long I have left of my final hour.

6

55 minutes. That's what the timer says, or at least it did a second ago. But now it says 0:54:59, and it's dropping constantly, which will continue to happen until the clock hits zero, and I'll be out of time.

And then I guess I'll die.

But while I still have time, I can't give up, plus I also have to question why my tormentor makes such a brazen point of showing me the minutes counting down, unless there was something I could do to stop the clock before it runs out?

Maybe there is a way out of this after all.

I just have to find out what it is.

'Tell me what you want me to do,' I say in a quiet and submissive tone. 'I'll do anything. Just tell me what you want.'

Even as I speak, I'm half expecting to be greeted by silence again, just like every other question has elicited the same response since this nightmare began, and I'm already preparing to speak again until I'm interrupted.

'I want you to sit here and watch the clock run down so you can see exactly how long you have left before I take your life.'

The pleasant surprise of getting an answer from this man is quickly overwhelmed by the horror of what he has just said to me.

'What? Why?'

I'm getting louder again now, but I can't help it. This man seems intent on killing me and even worse, he seems to be enjoying the process of it.

'Does the why matter?' he asks me, still standing only a few yards away from me, though he is just out of kicking distance if I was to swing my legs in his direction. That's annoying, although I should be grateful my legs are still untied, unlike my hands which are stuck behind my back, causing my shoulders to ache and my wrists to sting where the cable ties are rubbing against my skin.

'Of course it matters! I have a right to know why you're doing this to me!'

'I don't have to tell you.'

The calmness with which the man speaks is chilling. He's so still, too. Not flinching. Not shaking. No signs of nerves whatsoever. It's as if he does this sort of thing all the time.

Maybe he does.

I feel sick when I realise that I might be up against somebody who is so uncaring about human life that he could kill me and get on with the rest of his day as if nothing unusual has happened. If that is the case, then I really don't stand a chance here.

I need this man to want to negotiate. I need him to be susceptible to my pleas.

Basically, I need him to be human.

'Yes, you do!' I cry. 'You have to tell me why you want to kill me. I deserve that, don't I? Please, just give me that!'

I hate how pathetic and desperate I'm forced to sound just to try and get this man to explain things to me. I'm not used to being like this, and my behaviour is a far cry from how I tend to operate in life when things are more normal.

I'm cool, calculated and always in control. I have no choice but to be with what I do for a living. But I'm way out of my depth here, and it's showing by the strain in my voice.

'From what I hear, you don't deserve anything,' the man says, and he pulls out one of the chairs at the table so he can take a seat himself.

'Excuse me?'

'You heard me.'

'I don't know what you mean!'

'Have a little think. You've still got some time.'

He taps a finger against the edge of the timer, drawing my eyes back to the dwindling clock.

He's encouraging me to try and figure out why I apparently do deserve this fate, but I want him to give me the answers because that will be quicker.

'Just tell me who you are,' I say, my eyes watering slightly from all my shouting and straining. 'If you're going to kill me, then it doesn't matter if you tell me, right? I can't report you to the police if I'm dead.'

I'm hoping that rationale at least gets me somewhere with finding out the identity of the man behind the balaclava, but he just chuckles and shakes his concealed head.

'You're asking the wrong question,' he says after I've wasted five more precious seconds glaring at him.

'So what's the right question?'

The man sighs as if I'm somehow boring him with my right to live, before he removes his finger from the edge of the timer and rests his hands in his lap, once again managing to look effortlessly calm in the middle of a tense situation.

'I'm just somebody who is being paid to do this to you,' he says, his eyes looking me up and down for a moment before settling back on my face. 'The real question you should be asking yourself is who would hire me to do such a thing?'

7

The revelation that my captor is carrying out a job for an employer, like some kind of loyal employee who clocks in and out for a shift, is a startling one. It also means I might stand less of a chance of talking my way out of this if the person who really hates me enough to want me dead is not actually in the room and open to negotiation.

'Somebody put you up to this?'

I'm in disbelief. This situation is going from bad to worse.

Who the hell would hate me so much as to be willing to pay somebody to kill me?

A sigh escapes from beneath the balaclava, and this man is clearly not here for conversation. I'm sure he just wishes he could kill me now and be done with it, but for some reason, he has to wait for the clock to hit zero. That's lucky for me, but not that lucky.

'Wait, let me try and understand this,' I say, trying to think logically, and the first way to do that is not to keep looking at that damn timer, so I keep my eyes on the man sitting before me. 'Somebody paid you to kill me. So they made you put that letter through the door to what, scare me? What was I supposed to do after reading that? Stay here and wait for the hour to be up?'

'As I say, I'm just following orders.'

'They are very strange orders!'

The man shrugs. I guess strange is not something he considers when accepting a job.

'What's the deal with this hour?' I ask then. 'Why such a set time? And why give me a warning?

That letter and the timeframe gave me a chance to escape. I almost got away.'

Another chuckle from within the balaclava.

'You did not almost get away. But it's cute that you think you did.'

'I got out of the house. I could have made it next door to my neighbours. Then your plan would have been ruined.'

'But you didn't, did you? You're tied up in your home, and nobody is coming to help you, and when that clock runs out, you'll be dead. So stop thinking about how you almost got one over on me and spend more time savouring the last few minutes you've got.'

I really hate this guy. Not just because of the obvious fact that he is here to kill me but the way he talks to me. He treats me like a child. So condescending. Arrogant. Like he knows he always has the upper hand, and it's laughable if I ever think I might have it at any point.

But I'm right in what I said. I did almost get away. I was out of the house and in my garden. Maybe if I'd gone a different way. Turned left out of the door instead of right. I could have evaded him. Not walked into the trap.

The fact I feel like escape was a possibility for me, however fleeting the moment was, makes me think that this guy might not be as good at his job as he seems to think he is. There might be chinks in his armour. Weaknesses I can exploit.

This formidable foe might just be beatable. But only if I stay calm and use my brain to get myself out of this. And maybe I'll do that by starting with a little flattery.

'Okay, you're right. I wasn't close to getting away,' I admit. 'You caught me. Well done. I guess you're good at your job.'

'That's the first sensible thing you've said all night.'

'But seeing as how we're supposed to sit here for the next fifty-four minutes and ten seconds, how about we talk? You've got me right where you want me. I can't go anywhere, and I'm dead soon. Let's not sit in silence until then. Let's chat.'

'About what? The weather? The new prime minister? Whether or not England might ever win a World Cup again?'

I know he's being sarcastic, but the more I can keep him conversing with me, the better. Anything but him being silent and leaving me to stew in my own misery and fear. And the more he says, the more I can get to see the human side of him, the side that he has clearly made a big effort to conceal, what with his earlier reluctance to say anything at all as well as the fact he's covered his face.

He just mentioned a couple of banal topics like the weather and politics, but he mentioned something more specific. England and the World Cup. He's a football fan. Maybe I can use that somehow.

'Which team do you support?' I ask him, confident he'll answer that because it seems such a harmless question.

'What's that got to do with anything?'

'It doesn't. I'm just curious. I'm guessing you're a football fan. I am too.'

That last part is a lie, but he doesn't have to know that. I can just blag it. I just need him to keep talking, so hopefully, his tongue will be loosened so much that he'll eventually slip up and reveal more about who is behind all of this. And then I just might stand a chance of getting out of here.

'I'm a Chelsea fan,' he says before scratching his left arm, tending to an itch, which is something he probably takes for granted. I, on the other hand, am unable to scratch any of my itches with my hands tied behind my back, and that's just one of the many infuriating things about this ordeal.

'Chelsea. I like them. They're a good team, aren't they?'

'They're okay.'

'Do you go to many games?'

'What do you care?'

'I'm just trying to determine how much of a fan you are. Whether or not you're a true fan or just one of those glory hunters who only come out when the team might win a trophy.'

'I'm a true fan,' he says, and he sounds like he means it. He also sounds annoyed. More emotion. Good, I was purposefully goading him to see if he would take the bait, which he did. That's useful to know for when we're talking about more serious things.

'That's good to hear. You stick with them through thick and thin. I respect that. It's loyalty. And I always think loyalty should be rewarded. So let me try and reward it now.'

I wonder if that has piqued his interest. The fact he is staring at me suggests I have his undivided attention, so with that in mind, I go on.

'As you probably know, I'm a woman of considerable means. So how about I make you an offer? Whatever you're being paid to do this, I'll pay you more to undo it. I have money, and I'm willing to buy my life back from you. What do you say?'

A silence suggests he is considering it. But after a few seconds, I try and do a little more persuading.

'I'm sure you're being paid well for this job, but I can pay better. Big money. Life-changing money. You could do anything with all that cash. You could go and watch Chelsea home and away, all over the planet. England too. You want to see them win a World Cup? You can follow them to any continent and never have to worry about affording it. Let me buy my freedom, and you can have anything you want. What do you say?'

I'm confident that my sales pitch will at least have got him to second guess his actions and consider ditching his employer. There aren't many people who would turn down the offer of more money elsewhere, no matter how loyal an employee they might be.

'Come on, just say the word, and I'll give you whatever you want. You can turn that clock off, untie me, get very rich and then get out of here without me ever knowing who you were. How about it?'

I'm getting a little too giddy at the prospect of being able to talk and buy my way out of this situation.

I'm not proud of the fact that I can just throw money at a problem and magically solve it, but I'll do what I can to survive, and I'm pretty sure cash is my best chance of getting out of this alive.

He still hasn't said anything yet. He really must be thinking about it, which can only be a good thing. And then he picks up the timer and starts tapping on the screen.

The device is not facing me, so I can't see exactly what he is doing, but I'm hoping he's stopped the clock. Maybe he's typing out the figure that I'll have to pay him if he is to let me go. That's fine, I mean, he could just tell me what it is and save us a little time, but whatever. This guy clearly has a flair for the dramatic, so I guess we'll do things his way.

And then he stops and turns the timer back around so I can see the screen.

When I do, I'm confused. I can still see the timer, only there aren't as many minutes as there were before.

'What's that?' I ask him, confused as to what he has just done.

'That's the timer with five minutes taken off it,' he tells me. 'That's your punishment for trying to bribe me. Now, do you have any more offers to make me or are you happy to leave it and only have less than fifty minutes to live?'

8

I've never hated somebody so much in my life. All I want to do is get out of this chair, free my hands and strangle the smug son of a bitch sitting opposite me until he stops taunting me. Squeeze his throat until he gargles and gasps and begs me for mercy rather than the other way around. But I wouldn't relent. I'd keep squeezing until he drew his last breath, and I'd only let go when he was definitely dead.

But maybe he already knows I'd show him no mercy.

Maybe that's why he's showing me none in return.

The loss of five precious minutes is harrowing but not as harrowing as realising that I can't buy my way out of this nightmare. For a wealthy woman, I've rightly or wrongly become accustomed to using my sizeable wealth to get what I want. Cars. Clothes. This house that I'm now a prisoner in. But it seems I've found something that money can't buy.

My right to live.

'You bastard,' I say, my voice dripping in disdain. 'I was offering you money. I was trying to help you.'

'I don't want or need your help,' my captor replies coolly. 'And don't get it mixed up. There was only one person you were trying to help here, and that was yourself, just like always.'

It would have been a clever retort, but the last part of what he said piques my interest. *"Like always."*

That tells me he knows more about me than he is letting on and if that's the case, he might know exactly why somebody is paying him to do this.

'What do you mean like always?' I ask, praying he will elaborate. But he doesn't respond to that question, perhaps aware that he slipped up slightly a moment ago. But I'm not going to let him off the hook that easily.

'What do you know about me? What is it you think I've done that's so bad that I deserve this?'

'Shut up.'

'No, I will not! This is my life, and I have a right to know why you're threatening it!'

'Shut up, I'm warning you!'

'Screw you! Tell me what I've done wrong!'

'You've hurt people!'

There, I've done it. I've succeeded in getting my captor suitably wound up enough to give more away than he was initially willing to. But now that he has, it doesn't mean I'm feeling any better about things.

'I've hurt people? Who?'

I feel like I'm inching closer and closer to finding out who is behind this, but there's still some way to go yet.

'The person who paid me to be here tonight, for one.'

'And who might that be?'

'You must think I'm an idiot. I'm not telling you that.'

'Why not? It won't help me get out of here, will it?'

'No, there's nothing you can do to stop this.'

'So tell me.'

I'm so frustrated, but my captor seems to be getting that way too.

'Why should I?'

'I don't see why you wouldn't. If I'm going to die, then I might as well know what it's for. How else am I meant to regret it or say sorry?'

'It's too late for apologies.'

'At least give me some idea of who I've hurt!'

My breathing is heavy, and my heart is thumping, a result of spending the last minute shouting at the man opposite me. But it just might have all been worth it because as he sits and stares at me, he seems to be considering giving me what I want, which is an explanation. And then he speaks again.

'The very fact that you have no idea about who you might have hurt proves you have hurt many people in your time,' he says with a small shake of the head. 'Most people might have one enemy in life but you, well, I guess you have a few, don't you?'

'Enemies? I don't have any enemies?'

'No, of course not. You are just tied to a chair with less than fifty minutes to live because everybody in the world loves you.'

His sarcasm is just one of the many things I resent about him.

'Okay, fine. I have an enemy.'

'Just one?'

'I don't know. Maybe more. But I wouldn't call them enemies.'

45

'What would you call them?'

That's a good question, and I have to pause a moment before I answer it. 'Enemies' is such a strong word, so strong that I've never applied it to any of the people I've encountered in my life. But not all of those encounters have been positive ones, which means I have not always left people happier than before I met them, not that it was always my fault.

'Okay, so there might have been people I've had disagreements with in the past,' I admit reluctantly. 'But that's just life. Not everybody gets what they want all of the time.'

'Yet you seem to, don't you? Why is that?'

'What are you talking about? That's not true! I've lost things. I've been wronged. I'm no different to anybody else in that sense.'

Another chuckle followed by another shake of the head.

'Oh, you are different to everybody else. Very different.'

This man, with his balaclava, his knife and his infuriating ticking timer, clearly knows plenty about me. How could he say such things if he didn't?

Now he says that I am different.

It's funny because I always considered myself so, but in a positive way. I was different in that I was willing to work harder than most other people, different in that I sacrificed traditional things like a husband and kids to get to where I wanted to be and most of all, different in that I have achieved things that most only dream of. But now I'm being told that me being different is a bad thing.

'So what, I was supposed to be like the 99.9% rather than go my own way? Is that what I'm being punished for here? For achieving things? For working hard? For being myself?'

I expect an in-depth answer. More explanation. Clarification. Maybe a bit more of a debate. But I don't get that at all. What I get is a short and damning answer.

'Yes, that's right,' my captor says calmly. 'You are being punished for being yourself because who you are is pure evil. And deep down, you know it just as well as I do.'

9

Pure evil. That's how I've just been described.

Could there be a worse set of words to sum a person up?

Pure and *evil* together. How many others in history could be described in such a way? There are a few, but they mainly consist of notorious warlords and serial killers. But me, a businesswoman from the south of England who nobody outside of this part of the country has even heard of? How can I be put in the same category as all of them?

"Pure evil."

There has to be some kind of a mistake.

'What? You're joking, right?' I say, laughing nervously because I can't believe what I just heard. 'You think I'm evil?'

'I don't think it. I know it.'

'Then you're wrong!' I cry, suddenly switching from awkward laughter to desperate anger. 'I'm not evil! What have I done that's so bad?'

'I know what you're doing here. You're thinking if you can keep me talking, then I might start to feel sorry for you and give you a way out. But that's not going to happen. I've already said more than I should have, but this is where I stop talking and leave you to think about what you've done before your time runs out.'

The man stands up then, and after double-checking the positioning of the device on the table to make sure I can still see the timer on it, he goes to leave the room.

'Wait! Where are you going?' I cry, twisting my body so I can watch him walking away, but there's only so far I can turn my neck before my restraints cause me too much pain.

I get no answer, and now I'm left alone with nothing but the clock, the clock that silently and mercilessly continues to count down. I only have forty-eight minutes left now, and there's so much I have to do in that time. One, I have to figure out why this is happening to me and two, I have to get out of here before that man can come back and kill me.

I can hear him in my kitchen now. It sounds like he's rummaging through the cupboards. What is he doing? Is it not enough for him to come into my home and tie me up? He has to go through all my personal items too?

Then I hear running water, and I guess he's just pouring himself a glass of water. He's thirsty, but he's not the only one. I'm parched and can't remember the last time I had a drink. I guess it was the coffee I had in my car on the way back from my meeting in London.

The caffeine hit worked wonders then, waking me up after a busy day and keeping me going on my drive home, but its effects have worn off now. I've got a headache to go with my dry throat, although that could be caused by the stress of recent events more than anything else. Either way, my mind is feeling foggy at a time when I need to be at my sharpest.

Wriggling my wrists and testing the strength of my restraints again, I don't discover anything I didn't know a few minutes ago. The cable ties are still holding

49

me, making me a part of this damn chair and preventing me from using my hands to get out of here. But my legs are free, so what if I try and stand up. I'd still be handicapped, but maybe I can get mobile again.

I make an attempt at standing, but my arms are so far behind me that I can't get enough momentum to move forward and get to my feet. I guess my captor already knew that would be the case, which is why he didn't bother tying my legs together. Why waste a perfectly good cable tie when he didn't have to? Might as well save it for the next poor person he has to tie up.

I try to stand up a few more times, but it's pointless because I can't get anywhere, and all I'm succeeding in doing is causing my shoulders to ache more and my wrists to get sorer. I hear the tap go off in the kitchen, but no other noises follow, so I assume he's having a refreshing drink now, having peeled back a little of his balaclava so he can get the glass to his mouth.

I'm sure he'll have returned his disguise to its proper position before he comes back in here, whenever that might be. For now, I have nothing to do but stare at the timer, and it feels as though it's mocking me the more I watch it. Of course, it's not; it's just an inanimate object that doesn't care about me or the predicament I'm in.

In some ways, it's not all that different to the man in the kitchen, I suppose.

Staring at the timer, it's hard not to be overwhelmed by a sense of impending doom. But I force myself to try and stay positive, and one of the ways I can do that is by figuring out why a timer is being used in my ordeal in the first place.

One hour. What's the significance of that? Maybe finding that out holds the key to my survival.

So think, Katherine, think.

Somebody has given me sixty minutes to live. Somebody who hates me. Somebody who really hates me. What have I done in my life that could have caused somebody to want to torment me with a final hour?

It's very specific. It's decisive. It's a deadline.

And suddenly, I have an idea.

This is the first time I've been given an hour before something bad happens.

But it's not the first time I've given the same thing to somebody else.

10

THE EX-BOYFRIEND

'Pack your stuff and get out of here!'

Damian has never seen me like this, and I know that because he looks stunned by my outburst.

But what did he expect me to do after discovering his affair?

Tell him not to worry about it and suggest we order a takeaway and have a cosy night in? Of course I was going to react like this. Of course I was going to throw him out. And, of course I never want to see him again.

'You've got one hour to get your things together, and then I want you gone! You hear me? Gone!'

'Katherine, calm down, please. Let's talk about this.'

'There's nothing to talk about! You're a liar and a cheat, and I should never have trusted you. I won't make that mistake again because we're finished!'

I should leave it there, but my emotions boil over, and I end up pushing Damian away from me, my hands on his chest sending him stumbling backwards towards the bed, the same one we spent many a night lying in together before he went and ruined everything between us.

'Please let me explain! It's not what you think!'

There's no way Damian can seriously think he has a chance of talking his way out of this. The evidence against him is damning, and he knows it.

I found photos on his phone. Him with another woman. I have no idea who she is, but it doesn't really matter. I don't care what her name is, I just care that she was naked in half of the images, and Damian was in a similar state of undress himself.

Kissing. Cuddling. Doing God knows what else once they stopped taking photos and put the phone down. I don't need to know every gory detail. All I needed to know is that it happened. He's been seeing someone else, and now I do know about it, I can take action.

'One hour! I swear to God, if you're not out of my house after that, then I'll call the police!'

That might seem a bit drastic, but I mean it just as much as everything I've said in the last five minutes since I picked up Damian's phone while he was asleep beside me. Okay, so maybe I shouldn't have been snooping on his personal device, but I was only doing so because I had reason to believe he was up to something with somebody else.

My suspicions were first aroused when I saw a message flash up on his mobile phone while we were having dinner together in London earlier tonight. I'd got us a reservation at *Giodelli's*, my favourite Italian with sweeping views of the Thames, and while I've never been known for making romantic gestures, I had decided to break the habit of a lifetime and try and do something special for the man in my life.

It was halfway through the meal when I saw a message arrive on the screen of Damian's phone. He'd left his device on the tabletop rather than putting it in his pocket, but I wasn't particularly bothered about that because I know how busy life can be, and sometimes, phone calls and messages come through unexpectedly and need to be answered. Lord knows I'm never too far away from my phone at all times.

When I saw the message appear, I casually asked him who it was, assuming it would either be something to do with his work or a family member or friend getting in touch. But rather than answer me, he suddenly looked very sheepish and snatched his phone off the table before shoving it into the inside pocket of his suit jacket without telling me who it was.

If he hadn't acted so weird, then I would have just left it and gone back to enjoying my meal, but it was obvious he was a little on edge, so I pushed him on it, asking him to tell me who it was a second and then a third time. But he never did, and he tried to change the subject while chuckling nervously and fiddling with his wine glass.

I left it there for the sake of not making a scene in the restaurant, but there was no way I was going to forget about it, and I decided that I would check his phone the first chance I got. We've been dating for almost a year, and he's just given up the rent on his place to move in with me. That was quite the commitment on my part because I was more than happy to take things slow and steady, this being my first serious relationship and all.

Thirty-six is quite old to start dating seriously, but I'd always figured I was happier on my own, focusing on my career rather than dealing with the relationship dramas that other women my age seemed to be constantly doing battle with. But I made an exception for Damian, the handsome, cheeky guy who smooth-talked his way onto a date with me after we met on the train back from London to Kent one evening.

I figured I was finally growing up and even entertained thoughts of him being the one, proving it by letting him move in with me.

And then he gave me a reason to doubt him.

All I had to do was wait for him to fall asleep before quietly reaching over to the bedside table, picking up his phone and holding it just in front of his nose where the face I.D. would unlock his device for me and give me access. Once I had that, I checked everything.

Messages. Emails. And photos.

It was the latter where I found the damning evidence of deceit and betrayal.

It didn't take me long to kick Damian out of my bed, quite the rude awakening for him as he was pulled from his slumber and tried to figure out what had gone so drastically wrong in the short time since he had fallen asleep. But now he knows the game is up, and we are finished. And the deadline I gave him leaves him in no uncertain terms.

'Katherine, please, let's talk about this. Don't throw away what we have over something so silly,' Damian begs as I throw his shirt at him before looking around the room at what other things he has here that need to be gone.

Even though this is still technically my home, all of Damian's belongings came here along with him after he moved out of his flat. Clothes. Books. CDs. Not to mention a few toiletry items of his in my bathroom so he can have a shave and brush his teeth in the morning.

All things in my place that proved I was in an adult relationship.

But not anymore.

As Damian continues to beg for forgiveness and try and make out like this is all just some innocent misunderstanding, I scoop up one of his paperback books and launch it in his direction. The book, some awful autobiography about his favourite football player, narrowly misses him and hits the wall behind, but I've made my point just by throwing it.

I don't want to talk. I just want him out of here.

'One hour!' I remind him as I storm towards the bedroom door to give myself a breather away from him before I do something I'll regret. 'Whatever you leave behind after that will be going in the bin!'

'But I've got nowhere to go!' Damian says pathetically.

'I don't care. Go to her place. Or get a hotel. Just be gone within the hour.'

'There is no her. Not anymore. And all the hotels will be fully booked now. I'll be on the streets, and it's freezing out there!'

'That's not my problem. Just pack your things and leave or the police will be on the doorstep, and they'll make you leave if you aren't willing to go!'

I leave the bedroom and ignore Damian's ongoing protests, angry at him but even angrier at myself. So this is what I get for letting my guard down and letting someone else get close to me? Well, this is the last time I do that.

It won't be happening again.

I never make the same mistake twice.

11

Could it be? Could Damian be the one behind this?

Has he given me an hour like I gave him one?

As I continue to wriggle my wrists against the cable ties, I think about my ex-boyfriend and, more specifically, how he handled our breakup. He took it badly but then again, no cheat ever likes to be caught, do they? But it wasn't just the fact that he got caught that troubled him so. No, Damian really took the end of our relationship in a bad way.

I expected there to be some push-back when I told him he had an hour to pack his things and get out, and there was plenty of that. He kept pleading for forgiveness and refused to go, so much so that the hour's deadline passed, and he was still at my place, which meant I had no choice but to follow through with my threat and pick up the phone to call the police and tell them I had a trespasser on my property.

It was only once the call connected and Damian heard the operator's voice at the other end of the line that he realised I was serious about having him arrested if he wasn't gone. With that, he finally did grab his belongings and get the hell out of there but even then, he didn't leave without telling me that he would make things right and that we had too much of a good thing going on for me to throw it all away.

Of course, I hadn't been the one who had thrown it all away because he had done a pretty good job of doing that himself when he got involved with that other woman, but whatever. The main thing was that he was out of the house, and once he was gone, I was left to look around to see if there was anything he'd left behind.

The last thing I wanted was to stumble across reminders of the man I had once fallen in love with, so I completed a sweep of my home that night, removing anything that Damian might have accidentally missed in his haste to leave before the police got there.

I found a few stray items, like one of his self-help books about how to get a fitter body in just ten minutes of exercise a day. I did wonder at the time if the ten-minute exercise involved sleeping with a woman who wasn't your girlfriend, but I didn't bother turning the pages to find out. I just tossed it in the bin, consigning that particular self-help book to the trash where it most probably always belonged.

Maybe next time, my ex-boyfriend would be better served buying a book called *How to Keep It In Your Trousers For More Than Ten Minutes.*

I'd felt a little better after cleansing the house of him but only slightly because I still had the unfamiliar feeling of a broken heart to contend with. Like anybody who has been through such a thing, it wasn't easy, but it was even worse for someone like me, who was used to putting up barriers and never really let people in before.

Alongside the feelings of sorrow and regret, there were feelings of shame and frustration that I had allowed the chance of such a thing to happen to me. But I wasn't the only one going through some mental anguish because Damian was struggling too, and I found out just how much the following day when he unexpectedly turned up outside my place again.

I'd just got back from a busy day at work, and while it hadn't been easy to focus on my professional duties with my personal life in such disarray, I had also found that having something else to focus on had made a difference. But Damian had clearly not found the same thing because there he was, sitting on the wall near the front door that I had to walk past him to get to, and when he spotted me approaching, he leapt to his feet and launched into another impassioned plea for me to forgive him.

Thankfully, I wasn't that gullible and told him to get lost, just like I'd told him the day before. But he was even more persistent this time, not at all put off by us being outside where the general public could see or hear us, which only showed me how anxious he was to win me back.

He even got down on his knees at one point, right there on the cold concrete, and begged me to give him one more chance, not getting up when a dog walker passed us by with a surprised look on his face. I bet he hadn't expected to see such a sight when he'd decided to take his Labrador out for his walkies, and maybe he thought Damian was down on his knees to make me a wedding proposal.

But that romantic notion would have quickly been dispelled by me screaming at Damian that he was a pathetic loser and that I would report him for stalking me if he ever came back to my place unannounced again.

I didn't see Damian for a couple of months after that, and as I got on with my life, I presumed he had been doing the same thing. But that naïve assumption was proven wrong when I received a visit from one of Damian's friends, another unexpected encounter outside my home after a busy day at work and on this occasion, one that was so much worse than the first.

Rich, the friend in question, was there to tell me that Damian wanted to see me, a surprising statement because I had figured Damian had already wormed his way into another woman's bed by then. That was why I said no.

But then Rich told me where Damian was requesting this meeting from. It was a hospital bed where he was recovering from the consequences of the overdose he inflicted upon himself after failing to come to terms with our breakup.

I was shocked to learn exactly how bad Damian had been taking things since I left him, so bad that he had attempted to take his own life. It might have been his fault for us ending, but he didn't deserve to end up in hospital and certainly not to no longer be alive. I knew that, and Rich knew it too, which is why he urged me to go and see his stricken friend.

I should have said no. I should have left Damian to recover without me getting involved. Maybe what happened next wouldn't have happened if I'd just stayed away. But I felt bad, so I went to the hospital simply to offer my sympathies and wish Damian well in his recovery. But I was walking into an ambush because no sooner had I entered the ward and seen my ex-boyfriend lying in his bed beside several bleeping machines, then Damian went to work on getting me to take him back again.

He told me that he couldn't live without me and that it was my fault he was in the hospital, surrounded by other ill people who required the constant care of doctors and nurses to get them well again. I'll admit that maybe I had something to do with his overdose if he couldn't get over me but directly blaming him almost dying on me? That was cruel and very low, and I told him so, not that it made any difference.

Upon realising that my visit to him that day was as a friend and nothing more, he launched into a vile tirade of abuse, calling me all sorts of horrible names and wishing awful things on me, not least of which was death itself, a word I heard him use as I was being ushered out of the ward by a frowning nurse who had told me it might be better if I left.

But before I'd gone, I heard Damian say one more thing that sent a chill down my spine. He said that I would regret not taking him back, and the tone of his voice suggested that he meant it.

That was two years ago, and it took me a long time to forget it.

But I had forgotten it.

Until today...

'Hey! Come in here!' I call out to the man in the kitchen. 'I know who is doing this to me!'

I hope that will get my captor's attention and sure enough, it does because he returns to the room then, the balaclava still covering his face but his thirst presumably quenched after his drink from my tap.

One thing I notice when he re-enters the room is that he is no longer carrying the knife. He must have left it in the kitchen, and that's fine by me. Maybe he's getting a little lax the more I keep him talking.

'It's Damian, isn't it? My ex-boyfriend!' I cry. 'He put you up to this, didn't he? He couldn't get over me, and he told me I'd regret not taking him back. It's him, right?'

I wonder if my correctly guessing who it is might lead to me getting out of here. Will this man now contact Damian and tell him his cover is blown, and will Damian now be man enough to come and see me himself?

'How did you figure that out?' he asks me, making me feel even more confident about my prediction.

'It was the hour thing. I gave Damian the same amount of time when I threw him out. I guess he's returning the favour now. He must have thought he was being so clever with that deadline. But all he has done is given himself away.'

I'm feeling surprisingly smug for someone who is still in restraints, but guessing the identity of the person responsible for tonight is a victory for me, so I'm going to enjoy it. I enjoy it right up until the moment my captor chuckles.

'Come on now,' he says light-heartedly. 'Is your ex-boyfriend really the only person you've made an enemy out of?'

I hate him, and I really wish I could say no.

But damn him.

I can't.

12

THE CLIENT

'That's our final offer. Take it or leave it.'

I sit back in my seat and fold my arms to add extra emphasis to what I've just said, my defiant body language expressing just how much I am willing to walk away from this table if my demands are not met by the person sitting opposite me.

That person is Charlie McGregor, an astute businessman who has over thirty years' experience in being a part of meetings just like this one. But he doesn't have thirty years' experience in dealing with someone like me.

'Miss Wilkinson. I mean, Katherine. Can I call you Katherine?'

'You just did.'

I'm not about to allow myself to be charmed by this well-dressed, silver-haired company director, so he can use whatever name he wants. My first name. My last name. Hell, he can call me Princess for all I care. I'm not going to back down from my position, regardless.

'Okay, Katherine. First of all, I admire your fervour. It's great to see a woman like you have so much passion in the workplace.'

'You think being sexist is going to get you what you want?'

'I'm not being sexist. Perhaps it came out wrong. What I'm trying to say is that I commend you on how you come across, and it's clear your employer is very lucky to have you fighting their corner for them.'

I guess he's going for flattery now. Doesn't matter. It still won't change a thing, although I'm happy to sit here and be complimented some more before I leave this room.

'My next meeting isn't until this afternoon, so if you have more nice things to say about me and the way I do my work, then I'm all ears,' I say with a smile. 'But the offer I just made you does not change.'

I learnt a while ago that being stubborn might not be the best way to be in my private life but it sure can work professionally. State my position and then stick to it. That's how I get what I want. But, of course, the other side is always entitled to try and get what they want too, and Charlie is certainly going to keep trying.

And can I blame him?

I've just made him an offer, on behalf of my employer, to buy what remains of his company. To me, Charlie faces a simple choice. His company is slowly but surely going bankrupt, so he can either stay on a sinking ship or he can accept the offer I've just made him, an offer that will at least see him get some money for his failing business. But he hasn't accepted yet, and now he is about to explain why.

'You know, my great-grandfather started this company when he was in his twenties. That's a very long time ago.'

'Yes, it is,' I agree. 'But it's never wise to live in the past.'

'I'm not living in the past. I just want to respect his legacy.'

'Then respect this offer while there is still some semblance of a legacy intact.'

'You know I can't do that. The offer is far too low. The company is worth more, and you know it.'

'All I know is that your company is losing thousands of pounds a day and will continue to do so while you are in charge. So let us take it off your hands and see if we can turn it around before it's gone forever.'

I'm not saying anything that isn't factual, but Charlie still finds fault in my comments.

'You don't get it, do you? This company is a part of my family, and I wish it could stay in my family. But we've had some difficulties, so I am willing to sell. But only for a fair price, something your employer is not offering me.'

'The price is the price. Like I said. Take it or leave it.'

I've had enough of this back and forth and to prove it, I get up from my seat to show that I am willing to walk out of the boardroom.

'Wait! Where are you going?' Charlie cries before I've made it halfway to the door.

'I'm giving you some time to think.'

'I don't need time. I need a better offer. Please, I can't accept this as it stands. How will I be able to go home and look my family members in the eye if I sell everything we've ever worked for for such a low amount?'

'That's not my problem.'

'Have some compassion!'

I bet Charlie thinks he might be making a convincing argument by using such a word, but all it does is rile me up some more.

'I'm trying to do my job,' I say sternly to the old man in the chair. 'And compassion has no place in that, so I'd appreciate it if you would stop trying to make me feel guilty about this.'

'But you should feel guilty. You, your boss and everybody else involved in buying out companies like mine for such pitiful amounts. You're like vultures, feeding off the scraps of other people's hard work. You are profiting off people who are struggling. Does that make you feel proud?'

I grit my teeth and internally remind myself to stay calm. He is trying to throw me off my game. Get me to budge. Looking for a reaction. But I'm not going to give him one.

'I'll give you one hour,' I say calmly, retaining my composure. 'After that, I will come back in here, and you can either say yes or no to the offer. Either way, this will all be over then. I'll see you in sixty minutes, Mr McGregor.'

I walk out of the boardroom before the man at the table has a chance to say anything more, and by the time I return, I fully expect to get what I want.

And I do.

One hour later and the deal is finalised.

Charlie McGregor's company, the one that has been in his family for generations, is now owned by my employer. And now it has a chance of survival. But

Charlie doesn't see it that way, and I know that because after he has signed the paperwork and gathered up his belongings, he turns to look at me before leaving the room. When he does, I can see the look in his eyes.

It's different to the look that was there a moment ago when he signed on the dotted line. Back then, he just looked upset. But now he looks different.

He looks angry.

And he confirms it.

'How would you like it if I gave you such a short deadline to try and save what mattered to you the most?' he asks me. 'You think it's fair to dismiss over one hundred years of my family's company into a one-hour deadline? Shame on you.'

I didn't say anything to that. I just gathered up the paperwork and carried it all out of the room before handing it to the admin assistant, who scans all the documents and emails them to our lawyers, so they can make it all official.

And with that, another standard day at work was over.

13

'It's Charlie, isn't it?'

I'm convinced now that the man whose business I helped acquire for an inordinately low and, some would say, unfair amount is the person behind this. It could be him because he was a man of means, even after the loss of his business. Therefore, he could easily have paid for a hitman to come and see me tonight.

That makes way more sense than it being Damian, my ex-boyfriend, who never had much money to his name. But Charlie could have done this if so inclined, and the way he looked at me after he signed those papers in my office that day certainly suggested he hated my guts and blamed me for what had happened to him.

'And who is Charlie?' my captor asks, a tone to his voice that suggests he does know but would like me to elaborate, probably because doing so will make me feel very uncomfortable.

'Oh, come on, am I right or wrong?' I reply, impatient.

'I guess that depends. If Charlie is somebody you screwed over in the past, then I guess you could be right. But you wouldn't do that, would you, Katherine? It's not in your nature to screw people over, is it?'

I really hate this guy. He thinks he's being so funny with his sarcasm. But he's wrong to say such things.

'I didn't screw Charlie over or Damian! I was just doing my job when it came to Charlie. I was working for my employer. And Damian cheated on me. So please explain to me how I did anything wrong there?'

I'm very much convinced that I'm in the right, but sadly, the person standing in front of me does not seem so sure, and I guess he's the most important person to convince.

'You really think you did nothing wrong when it came to either of those guys?' is the next question I face. 'You can't see how giving them both an hour to do something they really didn't want to do was unfair?'

'What? No! Not in Damian's case, anyway. He betrayed me! He deserved to go, and I think an hour was too generous, if anything!'

'And what about Charlie? What did he ever do to you?'

I pause there because that's a harder question to answer. My tormentor is right. What did Charlie ever do to me? The truth is not much at all. He was simply another item on my To-Do list at work that day. Just another meeting in my busy weekday schedule. More of a task for me to carry out rather than a real person with real thoughts and feelings, or at least that's how I try to look at things anyway. But that's only because it makes what I do for a living easier.

'Okay,' I say with a heavy sigh. 'I guess I didn't behave impeccably when it came to Charlie. In hindsight, it wasn't fair for me to force him to make a big decision about the business he and his family had built, in sixty minutes. But what part of "it was my job" don't you understand? I had to do it, or I would have been fired and somebody else would have done it, can't you see that?'

Surely I was justified in my actions, right? But now the man in the balaclava is chuckling again.

'So that's how you do it, is it?' he asks me, sounding like he's got it all figured out now. 'As long as you feel like you have an excuse, then you can do anything to anybody without remorse?'

'What? No!'

'It sounds like that to me. You felt like you could just kick Damian out onto the streets with nowhere to go because he cheated, and you felt like you could be hugely inconsiderate to Charlie and his family business because you had a boss, so you just followed their orders without taking any personal responsibility for your actions. Wow, I guess things are quite easy in your world if you think like that.'

'No, it's not that simple at all.'

'So you do take some personal responsibility for the things you've done?'

'Yes, of course I do!'

My admission is a loud and passionate one, and while I can't see the lips of the man in the balaclava, if I could, I suspect they would be curled up into a smile now.

'Now we're getting somewhere,' he says, nodding his head. 'Well done. You've taken a very important first step.'

I swear I want to slap the condescending words out of his mouth, but unfortunately, I have to make do with just wriggling my wrists a little more before

71

ultimately giving up again. But I can use my own words, at least, to defend myself.

'Okay, I'll take some personal responsibility for what happened with Damian and Charlie,' I say, nodding too, but only because I have something else to add. 'But at what point do Damian and Charlie take responsibility for their actions?'

That question isn't answered as quickly, so I go on while I feel I have the upper hand, at least in terms of the conversation anyway.

'If you're saying that me giving each of them an hour to do something they didn't want to do was unfair, then okay, I admit that it was. But let's rewind and look at why I was forced into giving them that hour because if we do, I think we'll find they were the ones who started the ball rolling. They were the ones who ultimately landed themselves in that uncomfortable position.'

'Okay, I get it. Damian cheated, and Charlie had a struggling business. Is that still enough for you to treat them like they were nothing to you?'

'No, but it was a start and a damn big one,' I cry, passionate in my defence. 'I didn't make Damian message that other woman behind my back, nor did I make him get into bed with her and sleep with her in between telling me that he loved me and couldn't wait to build more of a life together. And I sure as hell didn't run Charlie's company for several years and oversee declining profits and numerous bad business decisions that ultimately forced them into having to sell what was left of their empire. So, yes, I made mistakes, and now that you mention it, I guess I do regret some of my behaviour back then. But if I do, then so should both of those men too, yet from what I can tell, they aren't the ones who are tied up in their own homes with less than an hour left to live, are they?'

I glare into the eyes of my captor, hoping now that he might understand that this is actually unfair, never mind a very serious overreaction to things I might have done in my past. But instead of admitting I might have a point before turning off the clock, untying me and ultimately, letting me go, the man in the balaclava just tells me something so frightening that I wish he'd never said anything at all.

'You want to know why you're tied up in your own home while those two men who also made mistakes are not?' he says calmly. 'Okay, then I'll tell you. It's because both of those men are dead, Katherine. And I know that because I killed them.'

14

I misheard him. I must have done. That's the only explanation.

He just said he killed Damian and Charlie. But that can't be true.

Can it?

'What?' I just about manage to blurt out, my heart thumping fast beneath my ice-cold skin.

'I killed them. They're both dead,' comes the simple reply, speaking so casually as if we're discussing what he bought at the supermarket the last time he was there and not the lives of two men from my past, who, despite what they might have done, definitely did not deserve to die.

'You killed them?' I repeat, growing more fearful by the second.

'What's the matter? You didn't think I was actually capable of murder? Well, I'm sorry to say it but you are sadly mistaken.'

He gestures to the timer again then to remind me of my own impending doom, and when I look, I see that I have less than forty-three minutes left now.

'But why? Why would you kill them?' I cry, the desperate urge to escape threatening to overwhelm me again.

'To prove a point.'

'What point?'

'That I am capable of taking another person's life. Maybe now you will actually take this seriously instead of still pretending like you can talk your way out of it.'

Is he for real? He killed two people just to make a point?

What kind of psycho is he?

And then I have a thought. Maybe he's just bluffing. Maybe he hasn't killed Damian or Charlie. He could just be pretending to try and scare me. Sure, it might have worked for a moment, but he can't fool me. He's faking it, and now I'm going to call his bluff.

'I don't believe you,' I say, forcing fake conviction into my voice. 'You haven't killed them. You're just trying to frighten me, but I know it's just a tactic. A psychological ploy. I know all about them because I do the same thing myself sometimes.'

'You tell people that you've murdered someone?'

'No, of course not!' I snarl back, not in the mood for more sarcasm. 'I just manipulate people. Find the right words to say to them that will elicit the response I need. Make them feel panicked or desperate or overeager.'

'Or rushed?'

God, he really is hung up on the idea of me giving people an hour's deadline. But whatever, he's right, I suppose, because that has been a strategy of mine over the years.

'Fine, yes, rushed. I rushed people to get them to do what I wanted them to. I did it. It was a tactic. But you're no different. You're just telling me that Damian and Charlie are dead to scare me, but I'm not scared because I can see right through you. In fact, if anything, I'm starting to pity you.'

'You're starting to pity me? But I'm not the one tied up.'

'But you are obvious,' I reply with a cutting smile. 'You think you're so slick with your words, but I know what you're doing. You're lying. And the ticking clock? That's just a visual representation of exactly the same deadline I gave to others. So all that leads me to think that you don't actually want to kill me at all when that hour runs out. Just like I did when I gave deadlines, you want something. All of this is just a smokescreen for whatever it is you want.'

For the first time since this ordeal began, I can actually feel the pressure around my chest lessening a little. Some of the tension also leaves my shoulders, and my heart rate returns to a somewhat more normal pace. That's because for the first time since I read that note that came through my door, I don't actually feel afraid.

I don't feel like I'm going to die at all.

Further boosting my confidence now is the fact that my captor is not saying anything to disagree with me. He's gone very quiet, and that is a sure sign that I've caught him out and exposed him and his lies.

'Can we stop playing games?' I ask him, shaking my head to show that we're both beyond that now. 'Can we just get to the point of whatever it is you want, so you can leave me alone, and I can get on with my night?'

I'm expecting a demand to come now and suspect it will be for money after all, because isn't it always? Therefore, I brace myself for having to make a rather expensive outlay, though I'm sure I'll be able to get it all back once the police have tracked down this chancer and got him to confess to all his crimes.

He's pretty good, I'll give him that, and he might leave here tonight with some of my hard-earned cash, but he won't get far. He'll pay for what he's put me through here tonight. I'll see to that.

'You think I'm playing a game?' he asks me, suddenly seeming like he still refuses to break character, and now he's taking out his phone again to show me something.

'Tell me, does this look like a game to you?'

He holds the screen in front of me so I can see the photo on it.

When I look, I see Damian's dead face staring back at me.

15

If I had the use of my hands, then they would immediately go over my mouth to stop the scream from escaping. But I don't, so all I can do to keep my emotions in check is close my eyes, turn my head away and refuse to look at the disturbing image any longer.

'What's the matter? I thought you said we were just playing a game,' my captor says smugly, but I keep my eyes closed just in case the photo is still on display.

I recognised Damian instantly, or at least what used to be Damian, but he looked very different to how he did the last time I saw him. Back then, his skin didn't have a ghostly pale hue.

Nor was it covered in blood.

'What did you do to him?' I ask, my eyes still closed but the image burnt onto my memory for all of eternity.

'I told you,' comes the response. 'I killed him. Just like I killed Charlie. Here, do you want to see his last photo too?'

I know I shouldn't look. I know I should just keep my eyes closed and pretend like there isn't a photograph being shown to me right now. But I can't help it. Part of me has to see, if only to know that he wasn't faking with the image of my ex-boyfriend a moment ago.

That's why I open my eyes.

And that's when I see that Charlie is just as dead as Damian.

Like the first photo I saw, the subject is lying on the ground, their body twisted awfully while their face is towards the camera, and their eyes stare straight ahead. There's blood on Charlie's torso, just like there was on Damian's, and both men look so helpless, as I guess any dead man would.

'What did you do to them?' I ask, closing my eyes again, though it's already too late because I've seen everything this killer wanted to show me already.

'I tied them up and then I stabbed them. Just like I plan to do to you when your hour runs out.'

I actually feel like I could be sick, and my next ten seconds, seconds that are extremely precious, are wasted with me doing my best to get the nauseous feeling to pass. I just about manage it, though it's only a minor achievement. I'm still tied up and still likely to die, so I'm hardly winning.

'They didn't deserve to die,' I say, stating the obvious.

'Some would argue they didn't deserve what you did to them, but life isn't fair, is it?'

Not this again. Is he really comparing what I did to them in the past to murder?

'Why did you kill them?' I have to know, opening my eyes again and feeling relieved when I see that he has put his phone away. 'Why not just kill me? Why did you have to hurt them?'

'I needed you to know that I was serious. I can't have you thinking that this is just a bit of fun because it's not. This is the real deal, Katherine. This is happening and the sooner you realise that, the sooner you might stop wasting your time.'

'Okay, so it's real!' I cry, whatever hope I had left escaping me again then. 'I believe you! You want to kill me! Fine, I don't have anybody, but Damian and Charlie? They had family! I met Damian's parents, and they were lovely! How could you take their son? And Charlie. He had grandchildren! What about them? How do you think they would feel when they find out their grandfather got stabbed to death by some lunatic?'

'They are not my concern,' is the cold-hearted response. 'Only you are, for the next forty-one minutes and thirty-three seconds anyway. Then, after that, I will forget all about you, just like I have already forgotten about the people I've killed in the past.'

It's impossible to believe that such a person could exist. How can somebody kill and not feel remorse? Never mind that, how can they just forget about them? It's beyond psychopathic. It's truly the stuff of nightmares. Yet such a person is in my home, just like they were in the homes of poor Damian and Charlie.

Oh good, those poor men. They must have been so afraid. So helpless.

And so confused.

'Did you tell them why you were going to kill them?' I have to know. 'Did you at least do them the decency of giving them an explanation? Or did you just butcher them without so much as a word?'

'Of course I gave them an explanation. I'm not utterly heartless.'

I scoff at that, even though it's not a funny thing to be talking about.

'So what did you say? Did you blame it all on me? I bet you did. It beats taking responsibility for your own actions, doesn't it?'

'Now look who's giving the lecture on taking responsibility. It was only a few minutes ago that you were blaming all your actions on other people. Do you even know what is right or wrong? Make your mind up.'

'I never killed anybody!' I scream, amazed that I even have to state such an obvious fact, but here we are. But maybe such a simple concept of going through life without taking another person's is foreign to the man in front of me, so I could do with spelling it out for him.

'A person in your delicate position should not be telling lies,' my captor tells me, confusing me even more.

'What?'

'You shouldn't lie to me.'

'What are you talking about? I'm not.'

'Yes, you are. You just said that you have never killed anybody. But we both know that's not true, don't we?'

Suddenly, it's all back again. The tight chest. The stiff shoulders. The erratic heartbeat.

That's because of what my captor just said.

Or rather, it's because of what he knows.

16

I've now decided that staying quiet might be my best bet. Why bother speaking anyway when this man seems to know everything about me? Surely it's better to say nothing and at least keep some blissful naivety about me having some secrets? Rather that than open my mouth and have him remove all doubt that he might not know something so personal about me.

He thinks I've killed somebody, and while it might have been completely different to his version of killing, he has a point. There weren't any knives involved in my experience, but somebody still died.

Somebody who absolutely did not deserve to.

And I was to blame.

I want to say it's not the same because it isn't, but I keep my mouth shut. While I do, the man in the balaclava, Mr Know-It-All as I might start referring to him, takes a seat again. He's clearly deemed this particular subject one that is worthy of him sitting down rather than standing over me like he has for the last five minutes.

'How does it feel?' he asks me after a moment. 'How does it feel to realise that we aren't that different, you and I?'

'We are nothing alike,' I snarl, breaking my vow of silence almost as quickly as I made it. But it had to be done. I can't sit here and have him make out like we are as bad as each other.

'Our actions have led to the death of another person, have they not? I'd say that makes us very similar. We could almost be friends, don't you think?'

I grit my teeth again, having done so so many times tonight that they are actually starting to ache.

'Do you want to tell me about the person you killed?' my captor asks me, but I don't answer because there doesn't seem to be much point. He obviously already knows about it and is just getting a kick out of trying to make me relive it. But I'm not going to give him the pleasure.

'Oh, you've suddenly lost your voice, have you?' he says with a snigger. 'No problem, I'm happy to do the talking for you. I'm happy to talk about your brother and his wife.'

There it is. Confirmation of the fact that he knows. Mentioning the two people who have haunted me for a long time.

I really don't have any secrets here, do I? I wish it was a freeing feeling. But it's not. Just like the restraints around my wrist, all it does is make me feel more trapped.

'Your brother,' he says again. 'What was his name?'

I'm not talking to him about this. No way.

'Oliver,' he goes on, answering his own question. 'But you always called him Oli, didn't you? Makes sense. Shorten the name. Make it sound a little snappier. Cooler, maybe. I bet he shortened your name too. Katherine is a bit of a mouthful. I bet he called you Kat, didn't he? Silly me, why am I even asking you that?

I already know that he did. That's because he told me so.'

I can't stay quiet any longer, not when I realise that he might have paid my brother a visit just like he paid Damian and Charlie one too.

'What did you do to him?' I beg to know. 'Please tell me you didn't hurt him! Please!'

'Relax, your brother is fine,' comes the response, and I never thought I'd be so grateful to hear this man speak. 'Well, he's alive, if that's what you're worried about. But he's not fine, is he? He never will be after what you did to him.'

Maybe it's time to go back to not talking again.

'How long is it since you last saw your sibling?' my captor asks, but he's not deterred from the topic when I fail to answer him. 'Over twelve months, I believe. Wow, that's a hell of a long time for a brother and sister to not be together, especially when they live in the same town as each other. Makes me think there must be a damn good reason why there has been such a long period of time without you two meeting up. Particularly when you consider that both your parents have passed away, so one might think that the pair of you would want to be around each other, just for a little comfort and support, if nothing else.'

I move my gaze to the wall to my left and keep staring at it, determined not to even give the man opposite me the decency of looking at him anymore, never mind talking to him.

'That's why you don't class yourself as having a family anymore, isn't it?' he goes on without the need

84

for eye contact. 'You do have a family member out there, but he never wants to see you again, so I guess you actually have nobody after all.'

I hate the fact that my eyes are starting to water slightly because I don't want this man to see that he is making me upset. But if I sit here and keep listening to him talk, then maybe I will cry. So desperate to avoid doing that, I turn to face him again and decide to speak.

'I love my brother,' I say with meaning. 'But I understand why he doesn't want to see me. I gave up trying to convince him that what happened wasn't my fault a long time ago. He wanted to be left alone, so I left him. That's it.'

'Except it's not as simple as that. It never is when somebody dies.'

'I don't know what you want me to say. That I'm sorry? Well, I am. I am truly, truly sorry. But I can't change the past, and I don't know what any of that has to do with what is happening now. Unless…'

The thought is an awful one.

'Unless your brother is the one who put me up to this tonight?' the man in the balaclava says, finishing my sentence for me.

I don't want to know the answer to that question and shake my head to make that clear. Perhaps to draw out my torment a little more, my captor doesn't give me a definitive response that would let me know either way. But he does tap the timer again.

'All we have established so far is that the concept of sixty minutes is important here,' he says as the seconds continue to tick down just below his fingertips. 'So, with that said, why don't you tell me exactly why an hour is so crucial when it comes to you and your brother?'

17

THE BROTHER

It's gorgeous. I know it'll look perfect in my living room.

I just need to make sure I can get it.

My fingers fly across the screen on my phone as I enter my bid for the green ottoman that has become available to buy for a very reasonable price on this online marketplace. I promised myself last week that I would stop making impulse purchases over the internet, yet here I am again, trying to buy something from a stranger to put in my home in order to make it look even better than it currently does.

I've worked hard on making my flat my own again ever since I kicked out my ex-boyfriend, and part of doing that has involved me buying all sorts of furniture items online. Lamps, chairs, even a rug that I ultimately ended up having to get rid of because it smelt of something foul that no amount of washing ever seemed to get rid of.

I definitely got addicted to buying things with my mobile phone, and how could I not when it's so simple? Just press a button, enter my bid and keep trying until I win. And I always win, probably thanks to my well-paid job, meaning that I am willing and able to go much higher than the other people I'm competing with. But now I've just seen something else I want, the green ottoman that I could use both as a footrest and a storage space, so now the bidding begins all over again.

But I don't have the time today to spend too long looking at my phone because I have several meetings lined up this afternoon. That's why I have gone in straight away with a very high bid, well over the actual asking price. I want to blow my competition out of the water and kill the auction before it's really got going.

I hope the seller will see my bid and just let me have it, and sure enough, I receive a private message from her thirty seconds after my bid has been made.

She thanks me for my offer and tells me that she will be happy to sell to me before asking when I would be able to come and pick the item up. She sends me her address then, and I'm expecting it to be local because I applied the filter on this website to only show me items for sale that were nearby. But then I see her address and frown because it appears there has been some kind of a mix-up.

You're in Margate? I type back, asking the question even though she very clearly used the word 'Margate' in the address she gave me.

I'm not, but the Ottoman is, comes the reply. *I'm selling it for a friend.*

I thought you were in Maidstone, I go back with because that's the area I applied to my filter.

Oh sorry! I should have made that clearer in the ad. But the ottoman is in Margate. Do you still want it?

I have to think about that for a moment because all of a sudden, the item of furniture I want is not nearby. Margate is an hour's drive away from my place, so it will be a two-hour round trip. Do I want it that much to sit in the car for two hours? Hmmm, it's annoying, but maybe I do.

No worries. I can pick it up this weekend. Is Saturday okay? Say 1 pm?

I'll have to re-jig a few things in my diary this weekend now if I am to make a trip to Margate, but it's no huge problem. Besides, the weather forecast looks good for Saturday, so it might be nice to be near the seaside. I could possibly make a day of it. Collect the ottoman, put it in my car, then go down to the beach for some sun and a bag of fish and chips.

No, sorry, it has to be collected today. My friend has builders at her house, and it's in the way.

The reply from the seller is even more annoying than the last one. Not only has she hoodwinked me into trying to buy something that isn't local after all, but now she is demanding that I drop everything and come and pick it up today.

Oh, that's going to be a problem. I'm at work now, and I have meetings until the early evening, so I can't get away.

I feel like that sounds fair enough. I mean, it is the middle of the working week. Of course, I have to work.

That's a shame. But it has to go today, so I'll have to cancel your bid and see if anybody else can pick it up sooner.

Alas, the response is not what I was hoping for, and now it seems I am going to miss out on the ottoman after all. Unless…

Wait a minute. I might know somebody who could pick it up today. Let me just ask them.

Leaving the app for a moment, I access my contacts before phoning the person I need to speak to.

'Hey, Laura! Hope you're okay!' I say when I get an answer. 'How's things?'

'Hey, Kat. Yeah, not bad. I mean, my feet are still swollen, and I felt a bit sick this morning, but apart from that, I'm all good.'

'Aww, bless you. Well, I won't keep you long. I was just wondering, and you can say no if you don't want to do it, but can you do me a favour? You see, I've just bought this ottoman online and-'

'How wonderful! Where are you going to put it?'

'Erm, my living room. But there's a problem. The seller says I have to pick it up today. As soon as possible, preferably. But it's in Margate.'

'Oh.'

'Yeah, and I've got meetings all day, so I can't get there. But I wondered if you could help me? Maybe go and get it for me? No pressure, you can say no, I just thought I'd ask as I know you're off work at the moment, and you said last week that you were really bored, so…'

'Errr.'

'Just say no if it's too much of a drive. I mean, it's an hour, so it is a bit of a journey. It's just you're the only person I know who might be free today. And if you could get it, then I'd make it up to you, I promise! Maybe take you shopping for baby clothes soon?'

90

'Erm, let me see.'

I hold my breath as I wait for Laura to make her mind up, but secretly, I am praying she says yes because I really want that damn ottoman now.

'Okay, sure, what the heck. I'll go get it,' she says, which is music to my ears. 'Beats sitting around the house all day going bored out of my mind. Can you text me the address?'

'Thank you! Yes, will do. I'll send it right now. And thanks again! I owe you one!'

The call ends before I go back to the seller and message her to let her know that I've arranged collection for today after all. She happily agrees to sell it to me then, so all I need to do now is send Laura the address, and she can go and get it.

I knew my sister-in-law would do this for me. She's such a lovely person, and besides, I'm kind of doing her a favour too here, I suppose. She's been on maternity leave for the last few weeks as her pregnancy nears the eight-month stage, and from what she's told me, she's never been so bored.

I know she's been driving my brother mad ever since she finished work and was even talking about going back to her office and working right up until the baby came. But he talked her out of that, telling her, quite rightly, that she should be resting now. But sitting in a car and driving to Margate isn't too strenuous, is it? By the sounds of her voice when she said yes, she's happy to have something to do this afternoon.

So that's it sorted. Laura will go and pick up my ottoman, and by the time I get home tonight, I'll have a new piece of furniture to put in my home.

Perfect.

My sister-in-law to the rescue.

How the hell was I supposed to know she was going to die that day?

18

The minutes on the timer have seemed to fly by since the clock started, but at this moment, it's like the seconds have suddenly slowed to a crawl. It's no coincidence that I feel this way because that's how I always feel about the concept of time when I think about Laura and my brother and their unborn child, who never did quite make it fully into this world.

'Laura died on her way to Margate to pick up your ottoman,' my captor tells me. 'Her car was struck by a lorry after its driver had fallen asleep at the wheel. She died instantly, as did the baby boy she was carrying.'

'Yes, I know!' I scream, the tears now flowing from my eyes and impossible to stop. 'You think I don't blame myself for her being out on the road that day? Because I do! I know it happened because of me, and I know I ruined my brother's life all over some stupid piece of furniture that I didn't even need!'

My captor nods, seemingly impressed at my admission. 'Well, at least you can be honest with yourself. Of course, some would blame it on the lorry driver and the fact he had been up all night after driving across from Europe, but that's just one small detail. The main reason Laura and her baby were there on that road at that time that fateful day was you, so well done for admitting that.'

I say nothing, simply sobbing, and when I close my eyes, I feel the bitter sting of my tears. I've cried enough over what happened that day, although for some people, my brother mainly, I accept that will never be enough.

'Tears can't bring Oli's family back, so dry your eyes, and let's not waste any more time.'

I open my eyes again to see the balaclava man sliding the timer across the table, so it's a little closer to me.

'We're coming up to only forty minutes left,' he tells me, though he needn't have because I can clearly see that for myself.

'So my brother is the one doing this,' I say, and it's less of a question and more of a sorry statement. 'He lost his wife and son after I sent them on an hour's journey to Margate, and he's never got over it, so now he's sent you here to kill me in one hour too. Fine, I can't even blame him. I'd hate me too if I'd lost everything.'

It's horrible to think that my sibling, the one I used to play in the park with and snuggle up on the sofa with to watch cartoons, has paid somebody to have me killed, but there is a lot that's horrible about what ultimately happened between us, and this is just the latest twist in a very sad tale.

I first knew something was wrong that day when Laura failed to reply to my messages asking if she had successfully collected the ottoman. Hours went by with no response, and I could see that she hadn't even read my messages, so I was getting a little concerned. But I had no idea something so tragic had happened.

I just assumed she was busy with something else. I even had the thought that she might have gone into labour, which would have been early, but I hear it happens, so I was starting to get concerned about her and my future nephew. That was why I called Oli to ask him if everything was alright.

When he answered, I knew from the sound of his voice that things would never be the same again. He could barely string a sentence together, but he managed to get out the crucial words in some semblance of a structure.

'Police…'

'Accident…'

'Lorry…'

'Laura…'

'Dead.'

I fought back against the strong wave of nausea that threatened to overwhelm me then and instead kept my composure enough to tell my brother that I was there for him and would be wherever he was as quickly as I could be.

He told me the address of the hospital he was at, and I took a taxi there immediately, leaving behind my workplace in London and eventually arriving at a ward that nobody ever wants to visit. It was there that I found my sibling, his head in his hands, as he sat on a blue plastic chair not far from where a couple of police officers awkwardly stood.

Oli was accompanied by who I later found out was a liaison officer who specialised in trauma and providing support to those affected by tragic events in the aftermath of such things. But the officer gave us a little space when I arrived, and as I sat down beside my brother, I put my arm around him and felt just how weak and vulnerable he was in that moment.

It took both of us a while to stop crying but when we did, Oli only had questions he needed answering.

'I don't understand where she was going,' he kept saying over and over again. 'Why was she so far from our house? Why was she driving? She should have been resting at home.'

Fortunately for my brother but unfortunately for me, I knew the answers to his questions, but it took me a while to give them. In those awful early stages, I wondered if it might have been better not to tell him why his wife had been behind the wheel and, ultimately, in the wrong place at the wrong time.

Did he have to know? It wouldn't bring her back, so what was the point?

What was the point of having him potentially blame me?

But I was also aware that leaving him to wonder for the rest of his life was cruel, plus there was the fact that there was the message on Laura's phone in which I'd sent her the Margate address, so he might find that one day anyway. That was why, after a few hours of wrestling with my decision, I told him why his wife had been on the road instead of relaxing at home with a cup of tea and counting down the rest of her days until their baby was born.

Of course, he reacted badly to my admission. I should have known he would shout and scream and blame it all on me. But I didn't regret telling him, and I figured that in time, once the dust had settled, once his poor wife and unborn child were buried, he would forgive me and blame the lorry driver more than me.

Maybe it would take a little longer than that. Maybe I'd have to wait for the lorry driver to be sentenced, which he was in the end, to four years, which was a pitiful term and nowhere near as much as he deserved. But even after that, even after another person had gone to prison for Laura's death, my brother still didn't forgive me.

And the last time we spoke, he told me he never would.

But he did speak to somebody else about me after that day. He talked with a journalist who had reported on the tragic crash and the subsequent sentencing of the driver, and in that interview, Oli said he blamed his sister for what happened.

It was quite the juicy story for the town's newspaper.

And it was quite the horrifying article for me to see on the front page of the papers when I went to the supermarket that day.

The journalist, if I would even be so kind as to call him that, did give me the opportunity of offering my own response, which would be printed in another article, but I just told him to get lost. The damage was already done. My brother had made it official that he hated me, and everybody in the town already knew it.

'This is his way of getting back at me,' I say solemnly to the man in the balaclava. 'I ruined his life, so now he's taking mine. I knew he was suffering, but I didn't realise he was this bad. But fine. Whatever he needs to move on. If he needs me dead, then so be it.'

All the fight has gone out of me now because while I would always vehemently defend myself about the things I did to Damian and Charlie, I can't when it comes to Oli and Laura. Hell, the lorry driver probably blames me too because if I hadn't asked her to go to Margate, then maybe his lorry would have just crashed at the side of the road when he fell asleep, and nobody would have been hurt. But what's done is done. And I guess one of the things that is done is that my brother has paid to make sure I am dead within the next forty minutes.

'Calm down, your brother is not the one behind this,' my captor says, shocking me because I had just convinced myself that he was.

'He's not?'

'No, he still hates your guts, don't get me wrong. But he doesn't want you murdered. He's not a monster.'

I'm so confused now.

'Why make me go through all that again if Oli has nothing to do with this?' I cry, furious that I was just reduced to tears for nothing.

'Because it's healthy for you to consider all the people you have wronged in your life before it ends, and just because Oli isn't behind this doesn't mean you didn't ruin his life with your actions.'

I don't know what to say now. I give up. I can't keep guessing or assuming or feeling guilty about what I've done in the past. I just want all of this to be over and given a choice between another forty minutes of mental anguish or just speeding things up myself, I know which one I'd prefer.

'Just give me a damn knife, and I'll cut my own throat,' I say, feeling so drained that I almost mean it.

I must surprise the man in the balaclava because he goes very quiet for a moment. But then he speaks and when he does, I wish I'd kept my damn mouth shut.

'Okay. I'll go and get the knife for you now,' he says as if it's as easy as that.

19

Is he serious? Is he actually going to go and get me a knife?

It sure looks that way because he's walking out of the room.

'Wait, what happened to forcing me to survive for the full hour?' I say, referencing the timer on the table.

'Well, that was the plan,' my captor says, pausing in the doorway and letting out a sigh. 'But if I'm honest, I'm getting rather fed up of listening to you, so if you want to speed this whole thing up, then be my guest. You'll save me over half an hour of hearing whatever sob story you have next.'

'You're the one who has been making me talk about those things,' I remind him. 'All I wanted to know was who was paying you to be here. I didn't want to go into detail about my past.'

'But you did, and don't you feel better about it for doing so?'

Best just to grit my teeth and say nothing to that. And maybe it's better if I just stay quiet and let him go and get me that knife. Sure, he might think I'm willing to use it on myself, but if I can get it in my hands, what would be stopping me from using it to defend myself against him? It seems unlikely, but he might just be about to hand me my way out, so I guess it's best to just shut up and let him make a mistake.

'Be right back,' he says, and he leaves the room then, giving me a moment to think about things.

My eyes still feel puffy, a result of the tears I shed over Oli and what happened with his wife, and I'm hardly in the best mindset to be thinking positively and considering ways out of this. But having been worn down mentally, maybe it's now time for me to get physical with my foe. If he does give me a knife, then there is nothing stopping me from plunging it through his chest, and given the opportunity, I won't hesitate to do so.

It's either him or me here, and I cannot go down without a fight.

Listening out, I hear the man in my kitchen again, and I'm envisioning him picking up his own knife or possibly selecting one for me from the drawer. But he can take his time and choose carefully all he wants to because that knife will be used to kill him, not me, so he can choose the biggest, sharpest blade for all I care.

I'm so busy daydreaming about killing the man who has put me through such an ordeal that I don't hear him making his way back until he's right outside the door. That's when I hear a loud skidding sound before he cries out and a second later, I hear what sounds like him hitting the floor.

Straining my neck, I try to see what has just happened in the hallway, but I can't see from this angle. Wriggling and wrestling with my restraints, I'm still struggling to find out what all the noise is about, but I do know that it has gone very quiet now.

But is that a good or a bad thing?

Realising that trying to swivel this chair around is not going to work, I have a go at rocking back gently to see if I can get a better vantage point that way. Leaning back very carefully, so the chair is on its two back legs instead of all four, I concede stability for the chance at seeing what's happened outside the door behind me. And as I lean back, I catch a glimpse of something.

A gloved hand.

I can't see anything else, but it looks like the man is lying on the ground. What the hell is he doing? He's not moving, nor is he trying to talk to me.

'Hello?' I say, my voice just loud enough for him to be able to hear me.

But I get no response.

'Hey! What's going on?' I ask, adding more volume to my voice now, but the outcome is still the same.

Now I'm really confused, and to try and curb my curiosity, I lean back even further in my chair. But I've overdone it, and despite attempting to correct my balance, it's too late.

The chair topples backwards with me still tied to it.

I brace myself for the impact and when it comes a second later, I let out a cry of pain. With my hands behind me, my shoulders have stretched back even further than is natural, and my first fear is that I might have dislocated one of them or possibly broken a bone in my hand or arm. But thankfully, I don't think I have because the pain quickly subsides.

But something has broken.

The back of the chair.

I'm still tied to it, but I'm no longer connected to the seat and the legs, and without being attached to that extra weight, I feel less trapped. I still have the cable ties around my wrists, but I can get them out from the back of the chair now, and even though my hands are still tied behind me, I'm free of the chair.

Rolling onto my shoulder with a heavy grunt, I begin the difficult task of trying to get to my feet, something that I can usually do easily but not so much now that my upper body is still contorted in an unnatural fashion.

With great effort, I'm able to get myself onto my knees, and after catching my breath again, I get myself to my feet until I'm now standing for the first time in a while.

It's not much, but it feels like a major victory, although I'm aware it will all be in vain if my captor comes in here and ties me to one of the other chairs. That's why I need to move quickly, but I also have to tread cautiously because I still have no idea what he is doing out there in the hallway.

Approaching the door as quietly as I can, I carefully peer through the doorway, trying to get a better look at the man. When I do, I see him lying on the marble floor, his arms splayed out to his sides and the knife he went to get lying harmlessly a few yards away from him.

He's not moving.

He might not even be breathing.

What the hell happened?

20

It takes me a moment to figure out how this man ended up on the floor, but I think I've got it. He slipped on the water that came off the bottom of my trainers when he marched me through here just after I'd been out in the snow. I guess he trod right on the melted ice and lost his balance.

I can see the wet trail beside him, and the irony of him slipping on the snow he manhandled me over is not lost on me.

But this serves him right.

Now he's unconscious.

Or is he dead?

My first instinct is to run, but what if he is just dazed and comes after me before I can get far enough away? Plus, the front door is still locked, so I'd have to go out the back again, and that didn't end so well for me last time. Unless I can get the front door key from him. He must have it on his person somewhere.

And I know what else he has too.

A phone.

If I can get that, then I can call for help and get the police on the way here. Hopefully, they'll arrive before he wakes up, and the first thing he'll notice when he does come back into consciousness are the handcuffs around his wrists.

The problem is that my wrists are still bound too, so it's unlikely I'll be able to get anything from his pockets. Maybe I am better just making a run for it. I could make it to my neighbours' house and get them to call the police for me.

I doubt they'll ask too many questions when they see me arrive flustered and with cable ties around my wrists. I think I'll make a pretty convincing prisoner. But to give myself an idea of how fast I am going to have to run next door and whether or not we might be joined by this man in the balaclava anytime soon, I conduct a test.

Tentatively touching the man's foot with my own, I nudge it ever so slightly to see if it's floppy or tense. The former would suggest he is unconscious or dead, while the latter might mean he is very close to waking up again.

But it's floppy. He is out cold and hopefully, never to wake up again. If he banged his head on the marble floor, and I'm guessing he did, then he might not survive that. I can't see any blood around, but there might be some damage internally. A cracked skull or bleeding on the brain; any of those things would reduce the chances of him getting up and coming after me.

It's time for me to get out of here, so I run to the back door again, praying it isn't locked so that I'll have an easier task at turning the handle with my tied hands. If I need a key, then I'm screwed and might have to find another way out, but fortunately, the door is open. I guess he was so confident of me not escaping again that he didn't bother to take precautions. Then again, he could hardly have expected himself to do something as silly as slip in the hallway.

But I knew it was always a risk because I've slipped there before, and as I open the door and get outside, I can scarcely believe I am breathing in fresh air again. I really thought I was a goner back there, fated never to escape my dining room and that damn timer. The timer will still be ticking down now, but I don't have to worry about it any longer.

It can hit zero for all I care because even when it does, I won't be dying tonight, not now I've gotten away from my tormentor.

Moving through my back garden as quickly as I dare to run with my hands tied behind my back, I reach the gap in the trees again. But this time, there is nobody waiting in the shadows to thwart my escape, and now I'm in my neighbours' back garden.

This patch of land is owned by Norma and Fred, a retired couple in their early seventies who I haven't had too many interactions with since I moved in here. That's mainly because I've been so busy, but whenever I have seen them, we've got on well.

I thanked them for the lovely welcome card they posted through my door, and I always wave if I happen to drive past them when I'm on my way to work and they're out at the front of their house. But I'll be seeing them in very different circumstances now, and I imagine they are going to get the shock of their lives when they see me standing on the doorstep looking like I've just escaped from an awful ordeal, which I most definitely have.

I hurry up the garden towards the house and notice there is one light on upstairs, which tells me they are still awake. It's still quite early on a Friday night, but they might have gone up to bed already, and I would hate to waste valuable seconds waiting for them to get dressed and come to the door, all the while I'm looking over my shoulder and hoping that the balaclava man is not coming for me again.

I'm halfway up the garden and already thinking about the first thing I'm going to say to Norma and Fred when I slip on the slope and fall to the ground hard, my face hitting the snow and knocking the wind out of me for a second.

'Damn it!' I cry, writhing on the freezing floor and wishing with all my might that my hands weren't so compromised. I cannot wait to get these damn cable ties off, and now that I've just fallen, I know exactly what the first thing is that I'll say to my neighbours when I see them.

'Get me the scissors.'

Drawing on my rapidly diminishing reserves of energy, I am able to get myself back to my feet and keep going, hating that I just wasted some time but relieved that I didn't end up hurting myself as badly as my captor when I fell.

Imagine if he came to and went to look for me, only to find me unconscious in the garden? I couldn't bear to make him that happy.

I reach the patio by the back door, and it feels good to be on much firmer footing now. But I keep going, moving down the side of the house and around to the front door because I desperately need Norma and

Fred to answer when I knock, and a knock at the back door will probably make them do the opposite.

Reaching the front door, I almost trip over the two small hedgehog sculptures they have by the doormat, which are cute but not so much when I'm in a rush and could do with fewer obstacles in my way, not more. I realise then that knocking is going to be problematic until I take advantage of the adrenaline surging through my body and use my head to do the knocking for me.

Hitting my forehead against the door, I make sure I make enough noise to rouse those inside but not enough to knock myself out. My skull is aching now but it's done the job.

I see a light go on on the other side of the door, and it looks like somebody is coming to answer my call.

Great. I'll be inside this house, and in a few minutes, I'll be free of these cable ties and speaking on the phone to the police. With a bit of luck, all of this will be over soon, and I can leave Norma and Fred to go back to whatever they were doing before I interrupted them so dramatically.

And then the front door opens, and I get a shock.

That's because it's not Norma or Fred standing in front of me.

21

'Who are you?' I cry when I'm met by the sight of the unfamiliar woman in my neighbours' house.

She's around my age with dark hair scrunched into a bobble and wearing a grey hoody and dark leggings, a casual look that suggests she is very comfortable here. But she doesn't live here. She is not Norma and Fred, and after so many shocks and surprises already this evening, I'm extremely wary now that I've just received another one.

'Who the hell are you?' comes the curt reply, and I guess her curiosity outshines mine because I am the one with my hands tied behind my back, after all. I'm also covered in snow after my slip in the garden a moment ago, not to mention my blotchy eyes from the crying and the erratic breathing that comes when one runs for their life.

'I live next door! I need to come inside because there's a man trying to kill me!' I explain, although that might be a slightly generous use of the word 'explain' because judging by the look on this woman's face, I have not explained anything.

I look over my shoulder to not only check that I'm not being pursued but also to reinforce the urgency of the situation to this stranger and when I do, she seems to get the message.

'Come in!' she says, suddenly ushering me into the house, and while I'm still on my guard a little because I don't quite know who she is, she can't be any worse than the person I'm fleeing from.

'Where are Norma and Fred?' I ask, looking around the hallway and up the stairs but not catching sight of either of them yet. All I do lay my eyes on is very antiquated décor and furniture. There's no marble on the floor here, just a floral pattern carpet, and in stark contrast to the staircase in my house, the one here is wooden and looks very rickety.

While it's my first time inside this house, I'd always assumed it wasn't quite as modern as mine, simply because the house I bought from Franz was a new build, whereas every other house in this area was built back in the 1960s. But even so, this place could do with some TLC. But right now, I don't care about the décor. I just need to know I'm safe.

'They're upstairs,' says the woman in answer to my question about the homeowners, and as she closes the door, I have the urge to tell her to lock it. But I still don't know who she is.

'Are you family?' I ask, assuming the obvious.

'No, I'm not.'

The door is closed, so at least the crazy guy at my house might have a harder time finding me if he is back on his feet and looking. But what is going on here?

'Are Norma and Fred okay?' I ask, looking around and feeling afraid that they might somehow have been dragged into this hell tonight too. My captor did appear from the bottom of their garden. What if he came by here first to silence any potential witnesses before he came to see me?

My paranoia is running riot, but I can't be blamed for that.

'Yes. Well, Fred is. But Norma is recuperating after a fall the other day. I'm her nurse.'

'Oh.'

I had no idea Norma had a fall, but how would I?

'What's going on?'

Fred's voice from the top of the stairs causes me to look up and when I see him, I feel relieved. Everything is okay here. There's no need to be paranoid. I'm safe now. Or at least I will be when that door is locked.

'Please, lock the front door,' I tell the nurse. 'There is a man out there who has been trying to hurt me.'

But the nurse doesn't move, and now it seems she is the one doubting me.

'Fred, tell her! I'm in danger, and I came here for help, but it's not safe yet! Please lock the door!'

Fred looks utterly confused, as he might well do to find his neighbour shouting and screaming in his home so unexpectedly, but at least he does what I ask.

'Lock the door,' he tells the nurse, and she finally does it.

'Thank you,' I say, relieved for all of one second before turning my attention to the next important task. 'Now we need to call the police.'

'Can you keep your voice down? Norma is trying to rest,' Fred says as he starts to make his way down the stairs.

'I'm sorry, but I'm just trying to keep us safe. There's a man in my house who was trying to kill me.

He slipped and banged his head, so I got away. But if he wakes up, then he's going to be looking for me, so we need to get the police here now!'

Fred reaches me at the bottom of the stairs and when he does, he sees the cable ties around my wrists.

'Oh my God,' he says, finally realising that I'm right to be so worked up here. 'Look at you.'

'I'm fine, but we need to call the police right now. Please.'

All the emotion of the evening is threatening to overwhelm me, and I don't have much more energy to try and convince Fred or anybody else of the peril I am in. How can they still be unsure after I've turned up looking like this?

'Fred, what shall I do?' the nurse asks him, obviously wanting him to make the call for her.

Fred thinks about it for a moment before he makes his decision.

'Go and get the scissors so we can get these cable ties off Katherine,' he says, shaking his head at my restraints. 'And while you do that, I'll call the police.'

22

'Thank you,' I say to Fred, grateful for the questions to have ended and for help to now be forthcoming.

'Come with me,' the nurse says as she passes me in the hallway, and I do as I'm told, following her into the kitchen, where I watch her open one of the drawers and take out a pair of scissors.

I hold my hands out behind my back as far as I can to give her as much space as possible to make the cut, but my shoulders ache terribly when I do so, and I wish she would hurry up and get it over with.

'Hold steady,' she says, and I do just that, and two seconds later, I feel all the tension in my bloodied and bruised wrists lessen.

The ties are off, and my hands are free.

Damn, that feels good.

'Thank you,' I say, finally able to bring my hands back in front of myself and when I do, I examine the damage that the cable ties have done to my skin. It's sore, but it shouldn't scar, so I guess I should be grateful for that. But what I'm even more grateful for is the fact I can hear Fred on the phone in the other room, and he is talking to the police.

'What happened to you?' the nurse asks me as she places the cable ties down on the table, probably leaving them out so the police can look at them when they get here. It's only then that I notice the name badge on her shirt. It says *Rosie*. A nice name to go with the nice profession she does for a living.

It's my first time being around a nurse since I was at the hospital with my brother after his wife's accident, and I'm just grateful that Rosie's uniform is not the same as the staff who were in attendance that day because I've had a hard enough time forgetting about those awful sky-blue shirts since I saw them. Or maybe it's just because they are part of what was easily one of the worst days of my life.

'Could I have a glass of water, please?' I ask, ignoring Rosie's question but not because I'm being rude. I just know I'll need to explain everything to the police when they arrive, so I'd rather be ready for that and not have to repeat myself too much.

'Sure.' Rosie fetches me the water quickly and efficiently, well-trained in taking care of somebody who requires her aid, and I think about how it was actually a stroke of luck that she was here when I came by tonight. Of course, it was bad luck on poor Norma's part because Rosie is only here because she had a fall.

'Is Norma okay?' I ask, concerned for my neighbour, even though I've likely been through the wringer even more than she has.

'Yes, she's going to be fine,' Rosie says as she hands me the glass of water. 'She was just a little shaken up after the fall, but there aren't any broken bones, thankfully, so she didn't have to stay in hospital for too long.'

'Thank you,' I say before taking a thirsty gulp from the glass and by the time I stop, I've drunk all of it.

'I'll get you some more,' Rosie offers, and she returns to the tap.

I receive my second drink a moment later and guzzle it almost as quickly as the first, and by the time I'm done, Fred has ended his call out in the hallway and tells me the police are on the way.

'How long will they be?' I ask, aware that every second might count if they are to catch the intruder in my home. Then again, when has every second not counted so far tonight?

'They're coming as quickly as they can,' Fred tells me, noting my bloodied wrists before averting his eyes.

I don't know whether it's a little of the shock wearing off or maybe the adrenaline is becoming less prominent in my body, but I suddenly feel a wave of sadness come over me, and tears fill my eyes again.

'I thought I was going to die,' I admit, without any sense of embarrassment or need to hide my emotions from the two people in the room. 'It was horrible.'

'Try and calm down a little. You're safe now,' Rosie says, quickly taking a seat beside me and putting a comforting arm around my shoulder.

I wince a little as she touches my aching muscles but it's not enough for her to notice and remove her arm, and I'm glad about that because at this moment, I really need the physical support. I've spent so long in my life thinking that I could do things all by myself, but in hard times, there's no denying it's the love of others that can keep a person going, and now I've survived this ordeal, I'll make sure to remember that in the future.

The brief silence that fills the room then allows me to hear the ticking clock on the kitchen wall and when I look up at it, I'm reminded of that timer in my dining room. I wonder what it says now, not that it matters. But until the police get here and have that man in handcuffs, I don't feel like I can fully forget about the fact that I was supposed to be dead within the hour.

And maybe I shouldn't, just in case this isn't actually over yet.

23

'I'm going to go and check on Norma,' Fred says, breaking the silence and preventing me from listening to that incessant clock on the wall any longer.

I watch him go, still feeling sorry for myself but also feeling a little sorry for my neighbour, who is obviously worried about his wife.

I wonder what it must be like to be married to someone for so long that they are so ingrained in your life. I bet Norma feels that she couldn't live without Fred, and I'm sure he feels the same way about her, which is why it must have been so awful for him when his wife had her fall and ended up needing medical attention.

Even though she is home now and has a nurse to call by and make checks on her, the worry is still plainly written all over his face, and I guess it will be until she makes a full recovery. In some ways, thinking about my pair of neighbours makes me feel selfish for worrying about myself so much tonight. But if I don't worry about me, then I'm not sure who will because, as my captor quite gladly reminded me earlier on, I don't have anybody else.

'Can I get you anything else?' Rosie asks me as we listen to Fred's feet plodding up the stairs.

'No, thank you,' I say, although the thought of whatever strong pills this nurse might be able to get her hands on is a tempting one.

My eyes are also drawn to the bottle of red wine on the kitchen counter beside the microwave, presumably a little treat that Fred and Norma afford themselves every now and again. But I should try and keep a clear head until I have spoken to the police, so pills and booze are off the cards, for now at least. But I'm sure I'll be calling on their sedating powers when I'm all by myself and trying to get to sleep at night back in the house in which I was so tormented.

'Do you know why somebody would do this to you?'

Rosie's next question is very different to her last few and reveals that there is more to her than just a nurturing side. She's obviously intrigued as to why a woman like me would force somebody to resort to violence. This is the suburbs, and I bet she hasn't encountered anything like this before. But she wouldn't be the only one.

'No, I've got no idea,' I tell her. 'All I know is that somebody paid that man to come to my house and kill me.'

'Oh my God, that's awful!' Rosie says, looking horrified as well she might because what I've just told her is barely comprehensible even for me, and I've already had the best part of half an hour to try and digest it. 'And you don't know who it was?'

I shake my head. 'Hopefully, I'll find out. But I need the police to catch that guy.'

'What if they don't?'

That's a good question and not one that I'd like to spend too long pondering. That's because the answer is surely an awful one. If they don't catch that guy and get him to reveal who was really behind the plot to have

118

me murdered, then can I class myself as safe? Or will I always be looking over my shoulder and wondering if it might all happen again?

'They'll get him,' I reply, hoping a little false bravado will settle my nerves.

I hear the floorboards creaking above my head and guess that it's Fred walking around. The bedroom that Norma is in must be right above us, and I wonder what he is going to say to his wife when she asks him what all the commotion is about downstairs. Good luck to him trying to explain this in a simple manner.

"Don't worry, dear. You know our neighbour, Katherine? Well, she just turned up with her hands tied and told us somebody was trying to kill her, but everything's okay now."

I can't help but laugh at my silly little daydream, and Rosie looks confused by that, but I don't bother telling her what I was thinking about. I just decide that fixating on my considerable problems is perhaps not the best thing for my fragile mental health so with that in mind, I focus on somebody else.

'How long have you been a nurse?' I ask Rosie, hoping that by the time she has finished telling me all about herself, I will see blue flashing lights outside and hear the sound of several uniformed officers entering my home and arresting the criminal that is in there.

'Oh, over fifteen years now,' she tells me.

'Do you like it?'

'Yeah, it's a good job. I mean, it's hard work but rewarding.'

'I can see that,' I reply and possibly for the first time in my life, I actually can. My focus in life has always been on making money, but without people like Rosie, where would we be in the world? I have no idea where I would be tonight, that's for sure. Probably still running around out there in the dark trying to find help instead of sitting here with a drink and a kind person to talk to.

'Did you always want to be a nurse?' I ask her.

'Yeah, I think I did.'

Rosie glances at the clock then, and I wonder if she's waiting for the police as anxiously as I am. Or is it because she doesn't like being asked so many questions? I guess it's the latter because she gets up from her chair then and heads for the door.

'I'm just going to go and check on Norma too,' she tells me, and before I can ask her to stay with me, she's gone.

I suddenly feel nervous. Maybe it's because I'm alone again for the first time since I ran from my house. I guess that would make me feel pretty vulnerable. Or maybe it's because I just got the sense from Rosie that she didn't want to keep talking to me.

That's not very nurturing of her.

But there's not much time to think about that.

Not when I hear the sound of something moving in the back garden.

24

My whole body turns cold as I listen to the sounds coming from the other side of the kitchen window.

First, I heard a twig snapping in the back garden.

And now it sounds like a watering can has just been knocked over.

I leap out of my chair and rush towards the back door to make sure that it is locked so that whoever is out there can't come in. But who else could it be wandering around in the back garden at this time?

It has to be him.

The man who wants me dead.

He must have regained consciousness and is now looking for me. If he's in Norma and Fred's back garden, then he's on the right trail. All he would need to do is get inside, and he would have me.

So I can't let him in.

I reach for the handle on the back door and pray that it won't move. If it does, then the door is unlocked, and I'll have nothing but my body weight to fend off the potential intruder. But the handle does not move and as I try it slightly, it still fails to budge. It is locked. Thank God for that.

But that doesn't mean we're completely safe yet. It's just bought us time, but I need to warn Fred and Rosie that we might be about to have company.

Rushing away from the door, I leave the kitchen and re-enter the hallway and as I do, I'm tempted to call out to those upstairs and let them know that we might be in danger. But I hesitate before doing so because making a load of noise might not be the best thing to do in this situation. That man out there might be listening, and if he hears my voice, then he will know for certain that I'm hiding in here.

I'll stay quiet and do my best not to give myself away if I can help it.

Knowing that the front door is already locked because I saw Rosie turn the key only a few minutes ago, I feel assured enough that the perimeter is secured as well as it can be down here, so I begin heading upstairs. But I creep extremely slowly, careful not to make any sound on the old staircase, still hyper-aware of that man outside and how he might have his ear pressed up against a door or window now, trying to make out the sounds of movement in this house.

I'm halfway up the stairs when I see a flash of light behind me, and when I turn around, I notice that the outside sensor light has come on on the front porch. It's the same one that was activated when I arrived at this house not so long ago and if it's on again, it can only mean one thing.

Someone else is at the front door now.

I stare at the frosted glass on the door and wonder if I'm going to see the shape of the man in the balaclava standing on the other side of it. Thankfully, I don't, but he must be out there if the light is on, so I hurry up, ascending the remainder of the staircase quicker than the first part of it.

Reaching the upstairs hallway, it's difficult to see much of anything up here because there is no light on, and all the doors are closed. But I can see a little glimmer of light coming from underneath the door furthest away from me, so I creep towards it, assuming that it's where I'll find the homeowners and the nurse, and when I get to them, I'll have to give them the startling news.

There is a dangerous man outside the house who desperately wants to get in.

And if he does so before the police get here, then we're probably all dead.

I have no idea how those in this room will react to that frightening news, but I have to warn them so we can make a plan, even if that plan only amounts to us all locking ourselves in the bathroom and hoping for the best.

As I reach the closed door, I take one last look over my shoulder, just to be certain that the man hasn't got inside already and followed me up the stairs.

But we're safe.

For now, at least.

I fumble for the doorknob in the dark before finding it and giving it a twist, and when it opens, I enter what is clearly Fred and Norma's bedroom. I see a large wardrobe to my left, one of the two doors on the front of it half open, revealing a rack of dresses hanging inside. I also see a dressing table with a mirror on top of it and an array of make-up laid out before it, clearly the place where Norma beautifies herself before any special occasion. And then I see the double bed right in front of me, the one with Norma herself lying in, or at least I think it's Norma because while I can see her hands laid across her chest, I can't see her face.

That's because it's covered up by the pillow being pressed down onto it.

The pillow is held by Rosie, the nurse who is supposed to be looking after her.

And while that is happening, Fred is just standing by the bed and watching on.

25

'What are you doing?' I cry, rushing towards the bed to try and remove the pillow as quickly as I can and clear Norma's airwaves.

Fred and Rosie are shocked at my appearance and clearly weren't expecting to be interrupted, but now that they have been, they try to explain themselves.

'I was just re-adjusting her pillow,' Rosie tries, removing the pillow that was pressed over the patient's face just a moment ago and putting it down beside the sleeping woman.

'You were suffocating her!' I say because that was clearly what was happening, and there's no point in her trying to deny it.

'Katherine, wait, you've got this all wrong,' Fred says, putting his hands out and doing his best to look like the sweet, innocent old man I once thought he was. 'We can explain.'

'Then explain!' I say, temporarily forgetting all about the danger lurking outside the house when there's clearly plenty of danger inside it too.

Fred and Rosie share a worried look, but there is no explanation forthcoming, and I'm not surprised because what could they actually say? I know what I saw, and they know I saw it too. They were trying to kill Norma and while I have no idea why, that's not really the point. The point is that they might just be as dangerous as the man who came to my house tonight.

'Get away from her,' I say, feeling like I have to defend the woman in the bed. Norma still hasn't woken up yet. Has she been drugged? Or am I too late and she's already dead?

'Katherine, calm down,' Rosie says, stepping away from the bed and moving towards me.

'Stay back!' I cry, pointing a finger in the evil nurse's direction. 'Both of you! Don't come near me, or I swear to God I'll hurt you!'

I point to Fred, too, to let him know that he's in just as much trouble if he tries to make a move as well. But he still has his hands out in front of him, and now that I notice it, it looks like he has tears in his eyes.

'It wasn't my idea. I didn't want to do it,' he suddenly says. 'It was her. She made me agree to it.'

He points at Rosie then, who has thankfully heeded my warning and kept her distance from me.

'Don't blame this all on me!' she cries, her voice loud enough to be heard by anybody downstairs, never mind in here. But still, Norma doesn't move. That's when I notice the pills by the bed.

'Is she dead?' I ask, afraid of what the answer might be.

'No, of course not!' Rosie replies.

'Because I interrupted you before you could kill her?'

'It was her idea,' Fred goes on, still pointing at the nurse. 'Norma did have a fall; that was true, and she ended up in hospital. Rosie was looking after her, but she told me she liked me. Said I was special and that she wanted to be with me herself. Then she said she had an idea about what to do with Norma.'

'This is nonsense,' Rosie scoffs, but if pushed, I'd say I'd believe Fred over her. There is a desperate honesty to both his expression and his tone of voice, whereas with her, she looks and sounds exactly like a naughty child after they've just been caught doing something they shouldn't be doing.

'I never should have agreed to it. Oh God, what have I done? I'm so sorry, Norma, I'm so sorry.'

Fred is in hysterics now, the enormity of what he almost went through with hitting him in waves, and it's obvious now that this elderly man was brainwashed into doing something heinous by this nurse. She must have targeted him. Saw him as an easy mark. For what? Money? His house? Certainly not love, anyway. But all the while we are being distracted by this, there is another problem lurking nearby.

'I don't know what the hell is going on, but the police will deal with it when they get here,' I say, glaring at Rosie as I speak. 'We just better pray that they arrive before that man outside comes in.'

'He's outside?' Fred asks, nervously looking towards the door behind me.

'Yes, he's outside! I came up here to warn you! Just before I caught you trying to kill Norma!'

'We weren't trying to kill her!' Rosie protests, but I don't have time for her lies now. I might have inadvertently saved Norma's life, but it will all be for nothing if that man gets in here and finds us in this room before the police do.

And then a sickening thought hits me, almost as hard as if I'd been hit by an actual truck. I turn to Fred with fear threatening to consume me and pray to God that the answer I am about to seek from him is a good one.

'Please tell me you called the police,' I say to him, suddenly aware that he might not have done if he was planning on killing his wife tonight.

He just stares back at me blankly, and now it feels like the four walls of this bedroom are closing in on me.

'Oh God, what have you done?' I say, my hands going to my head in exasperation. 'You didn't call the police? But I told you there was a man out there trying to kill me!'

'I'm sorry,' Fred mumbles as he looks at his poor wife in the bed.

'Have you any idea the danger we're all in now?' I ask him, but of course, he doesn't. He has no idea because he wasn't the one tied up to a chair earlier with a psychopath sitting in front of him. Neither was Rosie, the crazy nurse who is surely just as psychopathic as that man in the balaclava in her own way. But while she might target an innocent old woman who can't fight back, I'd say she will be no match for that man outside.

'We need to call the police now!' I cry. 'Where's the damn phone!'

'No,' Rosie says, suddenly lurching for me because she clearly doesn't want the truth about what she was about to do getting out. But there are more important things than her sordid little secret right now.

'Don't be stupid,' I scream at her as I look around for a phone. 'If that man comes in here, then he will kill us all! What part of that don't you understand?'

And then we all freeze when we hear it; the sound of breaking glass downstairs causes us all to look towards the bedroom door.

Then all that is left for me to do is state the obvious.

'We're too late,' I say, my voice now barely a whisper. 'He's already inside.'

26

'What do we do?' Rosie asks me now that she's finally realised that I wasn't exaggerating when I said there was a man who was coming to kill us.

'We need to lock ourselves in somewhere,' I decide. 'The bathroom!'

Rosie and I make a dash for the door, but Fred doesn't move.

'What about Norma?' he asks, and I turn back to see him still standing by the bed. 'We can't just leave her.'

He has a point, even if he was about to go along with a despicable plan only a moment ago. But what the hell are we supposed to do? Carry her to the bathroom?

I hear more glass breaking downstairs and know that every second counts, so I have to decide quickly.

'We'll turn the lights off in here and close the door,' I say. 'He might not see her and just chase us to the bathroom!'

'I don't want to leave her!' Fred says again.

'You are going to die if you stay out here!'

That seems to snap some sense into him, and he stops objecting as I hit the light switch and plunge the room into darkness.

'Come on, we have to go!' I urge the two people I now feel like I'm in charge of protecting, even though I'm not sure they deserve my help after what I caught them doing. But I can't just stand by and let them be killed, which they surely will be if that man gets his hands on them.

'Katherine! I know you're in here!'

The voice from downstairs turns my blood cold.

It's definitely him. My captor. *He's back.*

'Quickly!' I cry as I rush into the upstairs hallway before pausing and looking at the closed doors. 'Where's the bathroom?'

'That door at the end!' Fred tells me, pointing towards the furthest door from us.

We make a run for it but as we do, I glance down the staircase and when I do, I see an awful sight. The man in the balaclava is rushing up to meet us, and he's already halfway up the stairs.

'Quick!' I cry as I reach the bathroom door and push it open.

But I enter with so much force that I almost fall over, only just managing to keep my footing on the tiled floor. Looking back, I see Fred and Rosie entering the bathroom with me, and no sooner are they fully inside than I slam the door behind us and reach for the lock on the back of it.

My fingers desperately seek a grip on the small bolt, but they find it, and I just about manage to slide it across before our pursuer tries the door handle.

'Open this door!' he cries out, but that's obviously not going to happen, and I step away from the door, joining Fred and Rosie, who are currently cowering in the middle of the bathtub.

Just like the rest of the house that I've seen so far, the décor is very dated in here. A dreary shower curtain hangs down over a bathtub that has a faint waterline encircling it. The sink looks equally as unloved, the porcelain not exactly gleaming, while I notice the toilet seat has a small crack running across the top of it. Those are just the things I can make out from what moonlight is filtering through the bathroom window because we didn't turn the light on in here before we ran inside.

But it doesn't matter about that.

The main thing is that we got in here and locked the door before that man could get to us.

That same man is now slamming his entire body weight against the bathroom door in a desperate bid to break it down so he can reach us, and it's just another example of how crazy he is. It's also a sure sign of how angry and frustrated he is that I already managed to evade him once, and I'm sure he was disgusted when he woke up on the floor of my hallway with a sore head and saw the broken chair where he once had me tied up. But he's found me again now, and he seems keen to make up for lost time as he keeps slamming into the door.

But so far, the door is holding, although I'm not sure if it will continue to do so because, like everything else around here, I imagine the door was installed a long time ago. It could weaken at any time and when it does, the three of us in here will be like sitting ducks for the lunatic out there.

But what can we do? He's surely not going to give up.

Unless we can call his bluff…

'We've already called the police!' I cry out, trying to get his attention in between all the banging. Sure enough, the noise stops, and the door is left in

132

peace, for the time being anyway. 'That's right. They're on their way, so unless you want to be here when they arrive, I suggest you make a run for it!'

I glance nervously at Fred and Rosie then, wondering if they think I just did a convincing job with my lie. But it's only the person on the other side of the door who I need to convince, and as things remain silent for a moment, I wonder if he does believe me.

Maybe he has to? He must know that the first thing I would have wanted to do when I got here was get the homeowners to call for help. Of course, I had no idea that they weren't actually going to do that because they were in the process of committing a crime themselves, but the man in the balaclava doesn't know that either. He will surely think that we've already spoken to the police and told them all about him and what has happened so far tonight. So if he knows, the only sensible thing he can do now is run.

Right?

But there's still no sound coming from the other side of the door, and the longer things are quiet, the more uneasy I get about my plan working. Unless he's already left. Heeded my warning and ran for the exit, hoping to be long gone from here before the blue flashing lights turn up.

I'm just about to let out a sigh of relief and tell the two people hiding with me that I think we're going to be okay when I hear a floorboard creak out in the hallway.

He's still out there.

And what he says next proves that he is not going to leave us alone that easily.

27

'Open this door, or I'll kill the dear old lady sleeping in the bedroom,' he says coldly, without the slightest hint of emotion in his voice.

It doesn't take long for the three of us to realise that he has found Norma in her bed and is now using her as his way of getting us to unlock the bathroom door.

'Norma,' Fred says softly under his breath, and he instinctively goes for the door, but Rosie grabs his arm, stopping him from getting any closer.

'Wait,' she says, and I'm inclined to agree with her, even though it seems like we're in an awful predicament now.

Why couldn't he just have believed me when I said we'd phoned the police?

'You've got twenty seconds to open this door or I go back into the bedroom and kill her,' comes the ultimatum through the door.

'We have to open it,' Fred says, now fully back on board with keeping his wife in the land of the living and not having her nurse suffocate her so he could be with a younger woman.

'If we open it, then we die,' Rosie reminds me, still keeping a tight grip on his arm so he can't go to the door.

'But if we don't open it, then she dies,' he says, his eyes full of fear for the woman he once married.

'But that's what you told me you wanted,' Rosie goes on. 'So we can be together? But that will never happen if we open this door.'

'Tick tock,' comes the reminder from the man in the hallway, and I'm aware that time is almost up.

It's an awful predicament to be in, but in all consciousness, I know there is only one thing I can do here, so without giving it another moment's thought for fear of chickening out, I step towards the door and reach for the bolt.

'Wait!' Rosie cries, and I feel her hand swipe at my arm. But it's too late. I grip the bolt and slide it across, and a second later, the door is pushed open, and we're all forced backwards again as the man in the balaclava steps inside.

'Well done, I knew you'd make the right choice,' he tells me before turning his attention to the two people sheltering behind me.

But as he does that, I take my chance to inspect him and when I do, I can't see any weapon on him. There's no knife pointing in my direction, which makes me think I might actually stand a chance if I was to suddenly attack.

Lunging forward with nothing but sheer desperation powering me, I push the man backwards as hard as I can before screaming at Fred and Rosie to help me.

The man stumbles back, knocked off balance by the unexpected force I suddenly exerted on his chest, and as he reaches out for something to grab onto, his hands meet nothing but fresh air. He's now perilously close to the edge of the staircase, and one more push would send him falling down it, but he isn't quite there yet. Not unless one of us can reach him and give him that final nudge he needs to descend...

But neither Fred nor Rosie have come to help me, both remaining behind me in the bathroom, possibly frozen by fear or simply just hoping that I can get them out of this mess myself. But that's a lot to ask for, and despite my best efforts, I know I might not be able to manage to subdue this man on my own. The chances of that happening lessen even more when I see one of his hands grab the top of the bannister, and he manages to regain his equilibrium, clinging onto the top of the staircase just inches away from the top step.

I make a despairing attempt to reach him and push him again, but he's already moving out of my way and evading the danger of the staircase behind him. Now he's got the wall to his back and feeling more secure, I'm suddenly the one in danger of being pushed down the stairs.

He lunges for me then, and all I can do is put my hands up in front of myself and close my eyes, praying that whatever comes next will be quick and painless.

It turns out that it's quick.

But it's definitely not painless.

28

The pain caused by the blow to my head has me seeing stars, and as I fall to the carpet at the top of the stairs, I don't even have the presence of mind to be grateful that I didn't fall down the steps. I'm too dazed to know what is really going on, and as my head throbs and I struggle to keep my eyes open, I realise the danger I am in now is as real as it's ever been.

While I might have been tied up, threatened and chased, I've not actually been physically harmed yet.

Until now.

I can feel something running through my hair at the side of my head and suspect it is blood, though I can't confirm that because my eyelids are still heavy, and it's taking all my energy just to breathe.

My hearing is also affected - I'm hoping temporarily, as a result of the blow to the head I sustained, but for now, all sounds are muffled, making it even harder for me to figure out what is going on. I can make out somebody shouting and I think it's Rosie, but then the shouting stops, and I fear that it can't be a good sign.

A few more sounds mix in with the roaring in my head, and as I roll onto my back in the hopes that it will alleviate the aching in my skull, I wonder if the man in the balaclava is now working to silence the witnesses before he returns his attention back to me.

Fred and Rosie don't deserve to die here tonight, despite what they were doing earlier, nor does Norma, the poor woman who is still passed out in bed, or at least

I hope she is. They are just people who were in the wrong place at the wrong time, although I'm well aware that I brought this danger to their doorstep, and they wouldn't be in such peril if it wasn't for me.

But what was I supposed to do? I had a right to try and survive this, didn't I? But right now, it seems it's made no difference.

I'm still going to end up dead, regardless.

I briefly open my eyes, but all I see is the dark ceiling above me, and it takes me a few seconds to realise that the darting yellow lights I can see shooting around the lampshade are just the after-effects of the head trauma I suffered.

That man hit me hard, but I bet he could have hit me harder. The fact that he didn't means that he doesn't want me to die just yet. Maybe he really is keen to force me to eke out my final hour. But what about the others? He doesn't need to prolong their suffering, does he?

I try to sit up, but even the slightest attempt to lift my head off the soft carpet results in me feeling sick, never mind dizzy. I let out a groan, but the escaping of air from my mouth does nothing to rid me of the pain I'm in. I'm so disorientated that I briefly mistake the rails on the top of the staircase for bars and think that I'm in some sort of cage. But I'm not, I'm still just lying on the floor in the upstairs hallway, not far from the bathroom where I hoped to remain safe.

But I'm not the only one who isn't in there anymore because I suddenly see feet passing by my face, and it's obvious that the man in the balaclava is moving his prisoners.

I hear Fred pleading with the man as he passes me by, but Rosie is quiet, her white trainers scraping by the carpet only a few inches from my right ear, the only sound the nurse makes as she goes. I also get a glimpse of the balaclava man's boots before they move on, and it seems like they're all heading in the direction of the bedroom again.

Is he taking them in there to kill them?

'Stop,' I try to say, but my voice is barely audible.

I try again several more times, but each time is just as pathetic as the last, and I can't hope to stop anything if I can't even say a single word, never mind get back on my feet and try to help the others. I feel completely useless, just like I did when I was tied up in my dining room and crying over what happened with Oli and Laura. But this is even worse because I feel so weak now, and as I continue to languish on the carpet, I hear more shouting behind me from Fred before a door slams, and things go quiet again.

That's not all that happens because my eyelids grow even heavier until I'm forced to close them, and when I do, I feel like I no longer possess the strength to open them again.

Everything is black.

Maybe this is finally the end.

I guess I'm not going to last the full hour after all.

29

'Tick tock.'

The man's voice is close, so close that it sounded like it came from right in front of my face. Opening my eyes, it takes me a second to adjust to the light in the room but when I do, I see two eyes, only a few inches from my own, staring at me through the holes in a black mask. But the rest of the face is hidden, and that's when I realise that I'm looking at the balaclava man again.

'Wakey, wakey, sleeping beauty.'

He speaks again as his eyes seem to be examining my own. What is he looking for? A sign that I'm okay? Am I? My head still hurts from where he hit me. Or could I be dreaming? If so, this is a nightmare, right? But that idea is dispelled by what the man says next.

'Welcome back to the real world.'

Those words give me confidence that I am actually awake, so I try to move my body. When I do, my movements feel stiff, but it's a relief to discover that my hands aren't tied like they were last time. I realise that I'm sitting on a cold concrete floor, and when I move to get up, a hand on my shoulder keeps me in place.

'I'd stay where you are if I was you,' the man tells me, his face still close to mine. 'Unless you want me to hurt you again, of course.'

He moves away from me then and when he does, I get the chance to see what's behind him. It's a brick wall but that doesn't tell me much, so I look around and when I do, I see more of the same. I'm in a small room that I don't recognise, one that's about as big as what I imagine a prison cell to be like.

The four brick walls that surround me have nothing on them, and the only light is from a bulb hanging down from a wire above my head. And then I see the door. It's made from iron and has a small slat in the middle of it that can be opened or closed.

Maybe I actually am in a prison cell.

'Where am I?' I ask after failing to spot any discernible features in this room that give me some idea. The last that I knew, I was at Norma and Fred's. But it sure doesn't look like I'm there now.

'It doesn't matter where you are,' my captor tells me, walking over to the other side of the tiny room and leaning his back against the bricks. 'What matters is that the police will not find you even if they do come looking here tonight.'

I realise then that he still can't be sure that I didn't contact the police, although that doesn't seem to have helped me out much. Not if it's caused him to put me in this room, wherever it is.

'Then again, I don't think you did call them,' he goes on. 'I checked the phones at your neighbour's house and none of them showed any calls to 999. So I think you were bluffing earlier. I don't think anybody is coming to help you. But still, better to be safe than sorry. That's why I've put you in here.'

'Where are we?' I try again, but the man just shakes his head to let me know that it's not worth it for me to keep asking that question. So I try another one.

'What did you do to my neighbours?' I ask, dreading the answer because I'll never get over the guilt if they die because of me.

'What do you think I did to them?'

I don't want to say it out loud, but he must know that I'm thinking the worst, especially after he showed me those photos of Damian and Charlie earlier and what became of them after this man had finished with them.

'Relax, you don't need to worry about them right now. Just focus on yourself, you know, like you always have done before.'

The man goes to leave the room then.

'Wait! Where are you going?'

'I'm just going to get some fresh air. It's awfully stuffy in here, don't you think?'

He opens the heavy door then, and I think about making a run for it, but he's already closing it behind himself before I've even had a chance to move.

'Be right back,' he says before I hear a key turning in a lock.

Even though I know it's futile, I force myself to my feet to go and try the door. It takes a lot of effort because I'm still feeling groggy, and when I put a hand to the tender part of my head, I feel something wet. Looking at my fingers, I see blood. The wound is still fresh, so I can't have been unconscious for too long. Just long enough for that man to put me in here, I guess.

I use the wall to keep my balance once I'm on my feet and run my hands over the bricks, the harsh surface offering me no comfort as I search for any kind of weakness or vulnerability in this room that I'm trapped in. It doesn't take me long to examine each wall because the room is so small, and by the time I get to the door, I already know I'm not getting out of here unless I get lucky.

I pull on the handle but it doesn't budge because it's locked. I already knew that, but I had to try. The only thing left for me to do then is peep through the slat on the upper half of the door. When I do, I see a dark corridor on the other side. But it still doesn't give me much of a clue as to where I am.

But I do see something that I recognise out there, not that it's any consolation.

It's sitting on a small shelf on the right-hand side of the corridor and tormenting me just as much as it was the last time I saw it.

It's the timer.

And it's still counting down.

30

The return of the timer was surely not necessary. I could already guess that I was still going to die based on the fact that I'm locked in a small cell. But there it is, the numbers descending on the screen, taunting me with every tick and now that I can see it, I know exactly how long I have left.

Twenty-two minutes, which doesn't seem long at all, but considering I was briefly unconscious, it could have been worse. I might not have woken up until there were only a couple of minutes remaining, so I guess I should be grateful for that. Or maybe I was out for a while, and my captor has just made up the time remaining to further confuse and disorientate me. Maybe I was actually unconscious for over an hour, and I'm already living on borrowed time.

How the hell am I supposed to know?

'Hey! Can you hear me?' I call out, hoping the man is still somewhere nearby. But I get no answer, and he did say he was going for fresh air, so he must be outside somewhere now. That just leaves me languishing in here, but I'll be damned if I'm going to keep watching the timer anymore.

Turning back into the room that feels as if it's getting smaller by the minute, I try to make some sense of all this. Whoever is holding me has the capacity to have constructed a room like this, hidden away at the end of a corridor. Does that mean they purposefully built this room just for me? Or have others been kept in here before?

I'm not sure which answer scares me more.

But with little else to do, I decide to try and seek any clues as to whether or not other people have been kept prisoner in this cell in the past, and I do that by returning to the walls to examine them closer. I guess I'm looking for markings or something that might have been made by another person.

A name. A message. *Or even just some scratch marks.*

I don't find anything on the first wall that I check, but as I move onto the second wall and the one furthest from the door, I spot something. It's very small and around ankle height, so I crouch down for a closer look and when I do, I'm able to see what it says.

It's a name.

Karl.

Who is that? I don't know anybody by that name but the fact that somebody wrote that here must mean they were once imprisoned like I am too. I guess it's a male name, and my mind immediately begins to think about him and who he could be.

How old was he? What did he do to end up in this room?

And most importantly, did he make it out of here alive?

I quickly search for any more markings on the wall, wondering if I can find anything else that might help me paint a picture of the history of this room. Perhaps the key to getting out of here is knowing about its past, so I want to learn all I can about any previous prisoners. But despite searching high and low, I fail to find anything else that might help me. Just lots of unmarked bricks in neat rows, and by the time I make it back to the door, I realise that the one name written down low on the back wall is the only thing I've got.

I wonder if the man in the balaclava has seen the name down there. I assume he must have done but then again, if he's never been trapped in here himself, then would he have ever needed to go looking for it? Perhaps it's my desperation that led me to see it and now that I know about it, I wonder if it could be useful to me in some way.

If he knows who Karl is, and I have to assume that he does, maybe I can get him to slip up and reveal a little more about who might be behind all this. And a quick glance through the slat tells me I better be quick because that timer is still ticking.

But I'm not too worried about that because I know my captor won't leave me alone for long. If this whole ordeal has taught me one thing, it's that the man in the balaclava likes to be present to witness my despair. He sat with me in the dining room and conversed with me when he could have just left me alone, tied up with nothing else to do but watch the seconds pass by.

That tells me he can't help himself. He either likes the attention I give him, enjoys seeing me squirm or he simply wants to stay close to me most of the time so he knows I'm not getting away. The last time he left me alone didn't end well, with him slipping in the hallway and me almost escaping, so I'm surprised he's taken the risk of leaving me alone again. But then I hear footsteps outside, and I guess he is already coming back.

I move away from the door quickly so he doesn't see me peeping through the slat because I don't want to give him the pleasure of knowing that I've seen the timer out there. But I don't go too far because I'm wondering if I might be able to ambush him when he unlocks this door and re-enters the room.

Maybe if I'm quick, I could catch him off guard. Hit him over the head or something and then make a run for it. It's got to be worth a try.

As the footsteps get closer, I lean back against the wall to the left of the door and take a deep breath. This might be the only shot I get, so I've got to make it count.

Then the footsteps stop just outside the door.

I wait to hear the sound of the key turning in the lock again, but it doesn't come. Instead, I just see something being pushed through the slat.

It's a piece of paper, and I guess I'm supposed to pick it up.

With the door still locked, there's not much point in me waiting to try and ambush the man, so I reluctantly move away from the wall and bend down to pick the paper up. This feels just like the last time I did this, back when the letter came through my front door, the one that told me I only had an hour to live and started this whole nightmare.

As I unfold the paper, I see that there is another message for me written across it.

But this is even worse than the last one.

This one causes me to scream.

31

'No! You can't!' I scream as I rush to the slat on the door and look through it. When I do, I see the man in the balaclava picking up the timer.

'Hey! Look at me! You can't do this!' I scream at him, desperate for him to leave that ticking clock alone. All of a sudden, I feel like I need it because at least it offered me some semblance of structure. I always knew where I stood with that clock, or at least I always knew how long I had left. But based on the note I just received, that might be all about to change.

'Hey! Please! Don't do this! Talk to me!'

I bang my fists on the iron door, making an almighty din, but it's no good. The man continues to ignore me and only turns around when he has something to show me.

It's the timer.

And it's now turned off.

'No! What are you doing?' I cry, but it's all in vain as the man simply walks away, leaving me to cry out to him several more times until I'm certain he's gone and my cries are going unheard. Then I slump down to the floor, my legs suddenly giving way until I'm sitting with my back to the door and sobbing into my hands.

The piece of paper that was just pushed through the slat lies on the ground nearby, but I don't want to pick it up and look at it again. I already know what it says, so why torment myself further?

Change of plan. I'm just going to leave you locked in here forever.

That was the message, and that was why I screamed. It was also why I did everything I could to get that man to change his mind and not turn off the timer. I can't bear the thought of being left down here to die, dehydrating, slowly starving and eventually wasting away. It's akin to being buried alive.

So what if I've got a bit of space to walk around and stretch my legs? What good will that do me if I'll never escape this tomb again?

Given the choice, I'd rather have just been murdered when that timer hit zero. At least it would have all been over then. But how long will this nightmare last now? Days? Weeks? I don't know how long the human body is capable of surviving without water, but it's certainly enough time to cause me severe distress. I imagine I'll be in agony. I'll probably start hallucinating. But the outcome will still be the same.

I'll still die.

It's just going to take more time now.

This can't be it, I think to myself as I sit there sobbing. This can't be how it ends. I've fought too hard to just give up now. And what about my captor? All he's been through to ensure I didn't get away. All the things he made me relive. What was all that for if he was just going to leave me in here forever? No, he can't do that. This must just be another test, right?

My spirits soar slightly when I think that there might be a chance that I'm not going to be left in here for all of eternity. I'm desperate for any kind of hope to cling onto, so that will have to do for now. But then I realise that I can think whatever I want, though it won't do me much good if that man doesn't come back here and give me a chance to speak to him.

Forcing myself back to my feet while I still have the strength, I look through the slat, but there's no sign of movement out there. I can see the timer sitting on the shelf, but the screen is now blank, still worse than watching the seconds tick by. But why didn't he just take the timer with him if he didn't need it anymore? Why leave it there as a reminder to me?

No, he is going to come back. He has to. I just have to stay strong until he does.

I turn back into my cell then and look around and when I do, I remember the marking I found on the wall. The name. *Karl.* I should have said that name when the man was out there. Maybe that would have got his attention. I was too busy reacting to the note to think clearly. But that note is just a distraction, just like the first note that came through my letterbox and all the bad memories from my past that he made me recall.

Everything is done to confuse me and leave me second guessing, and whoever is behind all of this knows exactly what they are doing. They are trying to fry my brain, wear me out mentally and cause me to trust no one and doubt everything, even about myself. But I can't let them win. I have to try and stay one step ahead. I have to think clearly and not just react to whatever they give me.

From now on, I will not read any more messages that come to me, nor will I answer any questions I might get asked. It's time for me to take charge of this situation, and I'm going to do that by playing mind games with them.

And Karl is the key, I'm sure of it.

I don't think whoever owns this room knows that name is on the wall, which means they won't expect me to know about that person. But I do know, and what I don't know, I can find out.

I just need that man to come back, just one more time.

Come back.

Please.

32

While I'm waiting for my captor to return, something that isn't guaranteed but I pray has to happen, I decide to keep my mind occupied by attempting to figure out where I am. I fell unconscious after the blow to the head and was obviously moved during that time, but how? By car? If so, how long were we driving for? I don't remember hearing the sound of an engine but then again, I was out cold.

If I was driven, I could be anywhere now.

Am I even still in my hometown?

Then there's the question of who the hell has an underground cell they can keep people in? This is the kind of stuff you see in horror movies, which is why I stopped watching those when I was in my early twenties and realised I didn't need to frighten myself so much. But before I did, I saw enough films to know that some weirdos keep people locked away for fun, or at least there are some weirdos in the writing rooms of Hollywood who come up with that stuff.

Is the person doing this to me trying to recreate something he saw on TV once? Based on how secure this room is, I'd say they are well prepared, whoever they are. They must have some serious money, too, because who the hell can afford to construct a secret chamber with a connecting corridor? With that in mind, I try to think of anybody I might have made an enemy out of who has the funds required to do such a thing as this.

My mind instantly goes to Charlie, the businessman who was forced into selling his company to my employer. He was a millionaire. But I guess the key word there is *was* because, as the man in the balaclava showed me, Charlie is already dead.

Okay, so if not Charlie, then what about some of the other people who were forced to do things they didn't want to while I was in the room? Charlie wasn't the only one who had to sign paperwork handing over something he had built to my boss. I was always just the go-between. The negotiator. The middle woman, as such. But any one of those people could have held a grudge against me. I was only doing my job, but maybe they didn't see it that way.

But there are too many people to recall, too many faces to remember and names to try and dredge up. I'd never be able to confidently guess, and I might not even be on the right track. I only thought of Charlie because I specifically gave him an hour to sign his company over to us, and the concept of sixty minutes seems to be important here. Or at least it did. But the timer is turned off now, so maybe it didn't matter at all.

'Arghh!'

I lose control of my emotions for a moment, slamming my elbow back into the door behind me and instantly regretting it because it sends a jolt of pain right through my arm. I wonder if the man in the balaclava heard that. I certainly made a lot of noise. Or maybe this room and corridor are soundproof, and he's sitting somewhere else now, enjoying a cold beer, watching a game of football and trying to forget all about me.

No, he can't forget about me. How can he? People don't just lock other people up and forget all about them. Even if he is a maniac, he's not a machine. His thoughts will keep drifting back to me down here. And then there's the matter of whoever is paying him to keep me here. They'll want updates on my condition. They'll want to know how much I'm suffering. And ultimately, they'll want to know exactly how long I lasted before I died.

But how can they know those things if they don't come to check on me?

Unless they have another way of seeing me without having to come in here.

My eyes instantly look up to the roof of this cell then, scanning every part of it, searching the corners and the edges where the walls meet the ceiling. I'm looking for any deviation in the brickwork up there. Any gaps, holes or cracks. Anything that might offer the space to put something into.

I don't see anything ahead of me, so I turn around and start looking above the door. But there's nothing there either. Then I look straight up to where the bulb is hanging down towards me from a thin cable. Looking too closely at where the yellow light is hurts my eyes, but I force myself not to turn away because I need to examine the hole that the light's cable is protruding from. And when I do, I see something.

A faint, flashing red light.

Like one might see on a recording device.

Like a camera.

33

The realisation that I am on film and have been ever since I was put in here probably should make me feel sick. But it actually doesn't because while it is disturbing, it also gives me hope. It means I'm not really alone in here, not truly.

I have eyeballs on me. Somebody is watching me from the other end of that camera. My image is being relayed to a TV screen somewhere.

I still exist. I still matter.

So I still might have a shot at getting out of here.

I use a hand to shield the brightness from the bulb so I can look up at the red light for longer and see whatever device it might be attached to. Then I use my other hand to wave, making sure that whoever is watching me knows that I can see them now too.

I expect this will surprise them but that's the whole point. I want them to be shocked, and then I want them to come and see me in person instead of hiding behind a damn screen.

'Hey! I can see you!' I shout, still waving my hand above my head. 'I know you're watching me, you sick pervert!'

I have no idea if the viewer can hear me too, but it's worth a try. And calling them a pervert is just designed to irritate them if they can because they might not like that suggestion. But I don't mind being watched, not when it's a choice between that and being left alone forever. I also like the thought that my image is on a screen somewhere, possibly even being recorded, because that would all be evidence that would be very helpful to the police if they were able to get their hands on it.

I just need to get out of here and ensure that they do.

'What are you filming me for?' I ask now, still waving. 'Aren't you man enough to come out and see me for yourself? Why are you hiding behind a camera?'

I really hope they can hear me, otherwise I'm wasting a lot of potentially offensive words on nothing. But then I hear a sound outside my room, and as I spin around to look at the door, I hear footsteps approaching.

Yes, it worked! Somebody is coming! I knew they wouldn't leave me to die down here!

I rush to the door and peer through the slat and see the man in the balaclava back again.

'So I guess you found the camera,' he says to me as he stops a few yards away from the door. But I'm just glad to have company again, so I don't even care that he hasn't tried to unlock this door and come in and see me properly.

'What kind of sick game are you playing? Why are you watching me? And how long has that camera been up there? You put it there to watch other people too? How many people have you had down here?'

My questions come in torrents so fast that the man I'm firing them at barely has time to respond.

'And who is watching me? I know it's not just you, so who else is out there? Who else is getting a kick out of this? It's him, isn't it? The person paying you?

158

He's nearby, isn't he? Well, why can't he come out and say hello?'

I turn back to the camera then and wave again. 'Hello! Why won't you come and see me? What are you so afraid of?'

I've asked a lot of questions and so far, none of them have been answered by the man standing outside this room. But then he breaks his silence and does actually address one of them.

'You're right about one thing. You are not the first person to end up in that room.'

The statement is so casual it's almost as if he didn't just admit to keeping other people locked up in here before me. But I'm not as shocked as I might have been, and that's because of what I found on the wall earlier.

Turning back to face him through the small slat, I nod my head.

'Yeah, I figured that,' I say. 'A person doesn't construct a room like this just to use it once and surely not only for me. I know I'm not the first person to be locked in here. So, who else has been in here? And what happened to them?'

'I don't have to tell you that. It's none of your business.'

'But what difference does it make if you do? I'm not going anywhere, so why not indulge me? Tell me all about the poor people who died in here before I did!'

I hope that will work, but the man in the balaclava just shakes his head. 'No, I'm not telling you anything. Not yet anyway.'

159

He glances at the timer then, which is still turned off.

'Why are you looking at that? Does it still matter?'

No reply.

'Are you still counting down? If so, why did you turn it off?'

'To mess with you.'

The man turns to leave then, and I realise I'm losing my chance to talk to him much longer. That's why I blurt out the only thing I can do now, the one thing I have that might get his attention and alter my fortunes for the better.

One word.

One name.

'Karl!' I cry before the man can disappear down the corridor.

'Excuse me?'

It's worked. He's stopped walking.

'I know about Karl!' I say, which might be an exaggeration because I know his name and not much else, but it's a start.

'What do you mean you know about him?'

'I know he was locked up in here,' I say.

I hope that fact might cause more intrigue from my captor and he's still hanging around when he could have just left. But then he just chuckles and shakes his head.

'So what?' he says. 'Karl didn't get out of that room. And neither will you.'

And then he leaves, not even turning around when I keep calling out to him, and once he's definitely gone, I feel like I've lost my last hope.

That might be what causes me to consider doing something terrible.

The ultimate last resort.

But at this point, what else have I got to lose?

34

Returning to the centre of the room, I look up at the bulb hanging directly above me. I can't quite reach it with my feet on the ground, but I reckon I might be able to if I jump.

Leaping in the air might be quite a simple thing for an able-bodied person to do, but after all I've been through tonight, it's not that straightforward. I barely have the energy to be on my feet, never mind push up off the ground and jump into the air, but the bulb, or rather the wire it is hanging from, is the only thing I've got in here that I can work with.

I have to do it.

I have to jump.

And I have to hope that I can reach the wire when I do.

Bending my knees slightly into a squat, I push upwards as fast as I can with my hands outstretched above me, swiping at the wire. I make contact with it, and the bulb starts swinging wildly, causing the light in the room to no longer be distributed evenly.

I fail to get a grip on the wire the first time, and now it's even harder because it's moving, but I try again, leaping into the air, and this time, I get a firm hold on it.

Holding onto the wire and with gravity bringing me back down, the bulb lowers as more cable becomes visible. Now I no longer need to jump, I keep yanking on the cable until there is plenty of excess wire available, and I'm wondering if I might be able to dislodge the camera that is up there too. That doesn't seem to happen, though, but no bother because I have what I need.

Taking the cable, I wrap it around my neck, careful not to damage the bulb. Not yet, anyway. All the while, I look up at the camera so that I am making eye contact with whoever might be watching me. When I'm certain that they have seen me with the cable wrapped tightly around my neck, I take a deep breath before finishing the job.

I crush the bulb, instantly extinguishing all the light and plunging the room into darkness.

35

I don't know how long I'll have to remain in the dark with this cable around my neck, but I'm hoping it won't be too long. I think that because I imagine whoever was watching me on the camera will now be rushing to check up on me to make sure I'm not finishing the job myself and depriving them of the entertainment.

The last they would have seen of me before the light went out was me with the cable around my neck, and I'm hoping they take that as seriously as it should be. It looks like I'm going to harm myself and even if I'm not, they can't see me anymore anyway, so where's the fun in having a camera without being able to watch?

They'll have to come down here and check on me and when they do, I'll be ready.

There's only a tiny amount of light seeping into this room through the slat in the door, but it's otherwise dark, and I try not to let the inky blackness that surrounds me get to me too much. Yes, it's terrifying to be in a locked room and not be able to see anything, but I had to do something to get my captor's attention.

Surely they didn't think I was just going to be a good prisoner and go quietly, did they? Sit in the corner with my head in my hands and let them win? No chance. I'll always keep fighting for as long as I can, and as I think about that, I wonder what those who were in this room before did to fight back. People like Karl. Why didn't he try this? Maybe he did, and it just didn't work. Or maybe he didn't think of it and just accepted his fate. Unless he got out of here...

The man in the balaclava didn't even try to pretend like he didn't know who Karl was. I could tell he was surprised that I even mentioned his name. But he didn't say what became of him. Maybe Karl got away. That might explain why my captor didn't say much about him. It might be a sore subject.

It gives me great hope to imagine the last person to be in this room out there now in the world, living their life, free, enjoying the second chance they got after coming so close to death. Could that be me too? A second chance. Being grateful. Not taking anything for granted. Vowing to be a better person and not make the same mistakes as before? I'll kill to have the opportunity to find out, but until this door is unlocked, I'll never know.

But the darkness is all-consuming, and as I wait and pray for somebody to come and check on me, it's impossible to stop negativity from seeping in. When it does, I think about how unlikely it is that Karl did actually get away from him. If he did, then this room surely would no longer exist because he would have told the police about it, and they would have come to investigate it. They would have arrested those behind the heinous crime and made sure that nobody ever ended up in the same position again.

Wouldn't they?

Unless Karl didn't know where this place was. Maybe he just ran and ran with tears in his eyes until he was free, but when it came time to explain what had happened, he couldn't. Like me, he might not have seen the person behind all of this. How far can the police

165

really get with just a description of a man in a balaclava to go on? There's no way they could make any arrests solely based on that.

Even if Karl did escape, he might have been unable to make those who had done this to him pay. But I have to believe that he did escape. I have to think anything other than the alternative.

'Come on,' I whisper under my breath, praying to hear noise out in the corridor. 'Come in and check on me.'

I wait and wait for what feels like an eternity, until all of a sudden, I hear movement out in the corridor. Somebody is coming, but I make sure not to move yet because I need them to actually come in here and check on me. It's no good unless that door is unlocked.

'You think you're clever, do you?' the man asks me from the other side of the door. 'Well done, you've turned the light off. So what. You're still trapped.'

I say nothing, and most of all, I make sure not to move a muscle in case I am being watched through the slat, which I assume I am.

'Okay, Katherine, very funny. We can't see you on the camera now. Well done, you win. But I'm not opening this door.'

It actually feels good for it to be my turn to be the one who doesn't answer. Lord knows he's spent enough time ignoring some of the things I've said.

'What are you trying to achieve here, Katherine?' he asks me, and I see a torchlight come on. It's directed into the room and aimed right at me, so I make sure to close my eyes quickly and stay still. That way, all he will see is me slumped on the floor, my back to him, with the cable around my neck.

'Get up, Katherine,' he says.

I do not.

'Stop messing around.'

Again, I do not.

'Katherine? Can you hear me?'

I think that's the point where I really got his attention, and as I hear him utter a swear word under his breath, I guess he is suddenly not so cool after all. Then I hear something even better, something I was praying I would hear when I set this little plan of mine in motion.

I hear the sound of a key going into a lock.

36

'Katherine?'

I hear the door opening but maintain my position, knowing it's imperative to look as weak and vulnerable as possible, so the man in the balaclava comes closer to check on me.

With my eyes shut, I track every single one of his footsteps as he gets nearer, hearing his boots echoing off the concrete floor, and it's almost impossible to keep my heart rate relaxed as I do. But while my heart might be pounding in my chest, the man entering the room doesn't know that, and that's why he's coming inside to get a better look at me. For all he knows, I've harmed myself with the cable, and I might even be dead. But he won't know for sure unless he keeps getting closer…

'Katherine?'

His voice is right behind me now, and I bet if I was to turn and swing my arms, then I would hit him. But I don't do that because it's still too early yet. I need to make sure he can't fight me off and run back out of this room before I can get out first, otherwise I will have blown my chance, and I know there's no way I'll get another one after this.

'Katherine, if you're messing around, then he's not going to be happy,' he says, but I remain as still as possible.

And then I feel a hand on my shoulder.

Seizing my chance, I quickly remove the cable from where I was holding it in place around my neck and instead, loop it around the neck of the man behind me.

Pulling as hard as I can, I drag the man off his feet, and now he's on the ground with me. But I keep a tight grip on the cable and with it around his neck, I begin to pull even harder, suffocating his airwaves and causing him to gasp and gargle as the cable digs into his throat.

The torchlight he had has fallen to the floor, and I see that it was actually just the light from his mobile phone that he was using. But it's no use to him now, although the light is helping me see just how well I have got the cable around his neck and just how much the man is struggling to release it.

Revenge feels damn sweet after all this man has put me through, but I don't have time to savour it too much because the man is fighting hard, and as his body writhes on the concrete floor, his hands attempt to pull the cable away from his throat.

I'm trying as hard as I can not to let him do that, but it's difficult because he's stronger than me, and despite my best efforts, I feel like I'm fighting a losing battle when he gets a couple of his fingers under the cable and alleviates some of the tension that I was inflicting on him.

I grit my teeth and keep fighting, but I feel like I'm losing my dominant position, and if I risk it much longer, he might be successful in freeing himself from the cable, and then I'll really be in trouble. That's why I take a calculated risk and let go of the cable, surprising the man, who can now breathe again but is still very much out of breath for the time being.

Taking advantage of him still not being back to his best, I stand up and deliver a very hard kick to his groin, causing him to howl in pain and setting his recovery back considerably. And then I turn and run, rushing through the doorway before pulling the door closed behind me. It's not locked because I didn't have a chance to try and get the key from him, but all that matters is that I'm out of that damn cell, and now I can run for my freedom.

I race along the corridor, past the timer that was turned off when my demise seemed like a dead cert, and once at the end of it, I find another door. I'm overjoyed to find it unlocked and as I burst through it, I find a set of concrete steps rising up ahead of me.

Taking them two at a time, I bound up the staircase, well aware that the man right behind me would have recovered from the blow between his legs soon and be on my tail again shortly. And then I reach the top and find a hatch above my head.

Pushing up as hard as I can, the hatch opens, and I haul myself up before scrambling to my feet and kicking the hatch shut. There's a bolt on the top of it, so I slide it across, trapping the man down there and ensuring he can't get me now. But I know there is still somebody else I need to be wary of. It's the man who was paying him to do all of this to me so I can't relax yet.

I need to keep running.

Looking around for the next part of my escape route, I see an open door to my left, so I dart towards it, and as I pass through, I notice how thick the walls are that I'm passing through. Then I reach another door and as I push through that, I suddenly freeze because something is wrong here.

I need to keep running but I can't because I'm in shock.

I recognise this room.

It's my kitchen.

I'm in my house.

37

I know I should still be running as fast as I can to get away from that man, but I'm frozen with confusion. That cell that I've just been locked up in was underneath my house?

How?

And why?

But I snap myself out of it because I know I'm still in mortal danger, even if I am surrounded by home comforts, so I get myself on the move again. But this time, I'm not just going to run outside and hope for the best.

I need my car key, so I can drive out of here like a bat out of hell.

Rushing to the drawer where I put my car key when I got home from work earlier, I pull it open and am relieved to find it where I left it. If only I'd had the presence of mind to look for this earlier, then I could have just driven away and not gone next door. Then I wouldn't have got my neighbours involved with this.

Is Norma okay? What about Fred, though I'm less concerned about him after what he was doing with Rosie. Part of me wants to go and check on them because they might just be tied up and need my help getting free. But I can't risk being chased back there again because it ended so badly the last time I tried that. So I'm going to just try and get myself out of here, as far as I can, and I'll only stop when I'm at the police station.

Running towards the back door, I find it locked this time, but desperate and unwilling to stay here a second longer than I have to with that man behind me, I look around for something to break through the glass on the door with. Then I see the kitchen chair and figure it might be my best bet.

Picking it up, I contort my upper body before launching the chair at the glass on the door. It smashes through easily, and with my escape route clear, I use another chair to be able to step up and get through the space where the glass once blocked me.

Stumbling back outside, I waste no time running around to the front of the house, my feet slipping on the icy concrete below me, but I'll be damned if I slow down now. As I come around the side of my house and reach the driveway, I hit the button on my key fob, and the lights flash on my car, letting me know that it's now open. I also make sure to hit the button on the small electronic fob attached to my car key because that one activates the electronic gate at the end of my driveway and will open it so I can drive out in a moment's time.

As the gate slowly begins its process of opening, I reach for the driver's side door handle and am just about to leap in behind the wheel of my car when I notice something disastrous.

The front wheel on this side of the car is flat.

'No!' I cry, examining it further and seeing that it definitely has no air in it. Then I check the one behind it and see that it has suffered the same fate.

That bastard has flattened all my tyres.

I won't get far in my car now, so I need another plan, but as I glance back at my house, I know my captor could have broken through that hatch and be lurking in any of those rooms, ready to grab me if I go back inside. So I need to stay out here, which is why I take off running towards the gate, which is now almost fully open.

Skidding and slipping on my snowy driveway, I reach the gate just as it fully opens, and I see the main road on the other side of it. It's quiet, as it tends to be in this part of town in the evening, but just seeing the road and knowing that somebody could drive along here at any moment and help me is enough to keep me pushing on.

I glance back one more time at my house to make sure the man hasn't come out yet before I round the corner, but there's still no sign of him. Maybe he's still stuck in that room. Then again, when have I been that lucky so far tonight?

Rushing down the road, I lament the snow again because it likely means there is even less chance of a driver coming past here and seeing me and offering help. Anybody with any sense will be tucked up cosy and warm in their house this evening.

Only a fool like me would be running down the street without a coat on in these temperatures, but then again, only a fool would stay at my house when there was a crazy person inside it.

As I put some distance between me and my property, I have a few more seconds to think about the startling realisation that the underground prison cell I was kept in was a part of the home I bought recently. Of course, I had no idea it was there and would have had some serious questions for the estate agent if I had known, but it will be just one of the many things for the police to look into when they finally get here.

I see the lights from another neighbour's house up ahead and consider going to them to ask for help. But scarred by the memory of what happened last time, I'm still afraid because I still feel like I'm too close to my pursuer and he can track me. I really need a car so that I can put some real distance between us, and then I see the best thing I've seen in a long time.

Headlights coming right towards me.

I move over so that I'm in the middle of the road and then begin waving my hands to attract the attention of the driver.

They can see me, right?

The fear that I could be run over in a few seconds is suddenly very real, and I prepare to jump out of the way of the incoming vehicle, but then it hits the brakes.

They're stopping for me!

'Help me!' I cry, running towards the driver's side door, and as they wind their window down, I see a woman in a woollen hat looking out at me as if I'm mad.

'Help! There's a man chasing me! He's at my house! We need to go right now!'

The woman is stunned, but there's no time to explain and when she doesn't protest, I open the door behind her and get in.

The warmth in the car is a relief to my freezing bones, and as I put my seatbelt on, I tell the woman where we need to go next.

'The police station! Quick!'

I should perhaps be a little more polite or try and give a bit of information about what is going on, but the driver seems to need little convincing and puts the car back in motion. I guess a distressed woman running down the road at this time on a Friday night does not need explaining. It just needs action, and now we're moving, I feel much better.

But going in this direction means we'll pass my house again in a moment, and I wonder if I'll catch a glimpse of that man in the balaclava when we do. If he's made it out of that cell and if he's got any sense, then he will have made a run for it himself now, so hopefully, he's long gone. But just to be safe, I slide down in my seat so that he wouldn't be able to see me if he is out here when we drive past.

I see the open gate at the top of my driveway, and then my useless car comes into view. But there's no sign of the man. I've really got away.

And then, inexplicably, my driver slows down.

Just before she turns the car back onto my driveway.

38

'Wait! What are you doing?' I cry out, leaning forward on the back seat to be closer to the driver so I can warn her about the danger she has just put us in. 'He's here! This is my house! We need to go now before he finds us!'

But the driver says nothing. All she does is park the car, so we're now sitting just behind my car.

'Hey! What the hell are you doing?'

I feel like I could hit her. Maybe I need to in order to slap some sense into her. But I don't because she is doing me a favour and helped me a moment ago. But she's not helping me right now.

'This is where I was running from!' I try and explain to her. 'There's a man in that house, and he is trying to kill me! We need to leave before he comes out, or you'll be in danger too!'

Surely I can't make myself any clearer than that, and I expect the driver to put the vehicle in reverse and get us out of here. But she doesn't do that.

She simply turns the engine off and takes the key out of the ignition.

'Hey! Can you hear me? We're in danger!'

I'm starting to wonder if this woman is deaf. That's the only explanation for her willingly putting us back in harm's way. But then she does something else, something that changes the whole dynamic of this journey.

She locks the doors, so I can't get out.

That's when I realise that I have made a big mistake getting inside this car.

39

'Let me out!' I cry as I pull on the door handle beside me, but it's no good.

I'm trapped.

But who am I trapped with?

Looking at the reflection in the rearview mirror hanging above the steering wheel, I see the eyes of the female driver staring back at me. But I don't recognise her, nor is she saying anything that might give me a clue as to why she is doing this to me. She's just sitting there. She looks so calm. But beneath that placid veneer, there is obviously a dangerous woman lurking.

One that I need to get away from as quickly as I can.

'Let me out!' I cry again, raising my hand to strike the woman who is obviously not on my side after all. But she grabs my wrist just before I can hit her before twisting it and causing me to howl out in pain. Still holding onto my limb that is now in a very awkward position, she looks out through the windscreen, and when I follow her gaze, I see what she does.

The man in the balaclava approaching the car.

'No!' I cry, yanking my arm away from her, and I manage to break free, but that's not much good because I'm still stuck inside the car. Now that man is out there, do I even want to get out anymore?

It doesn't matter what I want because I hear the car doors unlocking before the passenger door is pulled open, and a gloved hand reaches in to grab me.

'No!' I cry, trying to fend the hand off, but then it grabs a bunch of my hair, and I'm pulled out of the vehicle. I'm forced to go along with it or lose my hair, and once I'm back on the driveway, the man in the balaclava clamps his hand over my mouth to stop me from making another sound.

Then he drags me back towards the house, and while I do my best to drag my feet and slow him down, he's overpowering me.

As I go, I look back towards the car, wondering what the woman at the wheel might be doing while all of this is going on. But I wish I hadn't because when I see her, I get confirmation that she is as much a part of this evil plot as the man currently holding on to me.

The woman is watching me being dragged away.

And she is smiling.

I'm bundled back into the house and dragged into the living room before being pushed onto one of my sofas. But before I even think about getting back and trying to make another run for it-

'Stay there!' the man in the balaclava shouts, and this time, I'm inclined to do as he says because he has just brandished another weapon.

But it's not a knife this time.

It's a gun.

I stare at the end of the barrel that's pointed in my direction before noting the man's index finger curled around the trigger. He is ready to shoot if he needs to, so I better not test his aim. But it might not even be up to me anymore because after strangling him with the cable in that cell and making it out of this house, he surely has enough motivation to pull that trigger without me adding to it.

The man's eyes bore into me and while I can't see the rest of his expression, I expect it is one of anger. That's why I close my eyes and expect this to be over any second now. He is surely going to kill me. What else could he be waiting for?

'Katherine. It's good to have you back with us.'

I open my eyes at the sound of a voice, a voice I don't recognise, and when I do, I see another man has entered the room. He's standing beside the guy with the itchy trigger finger, but who is he?

And why has he got a German accent?

'Put that down,' he tells his partner with the weapon. 'We don't need that. Not yet, anyway.'

The gun is eventually lowered, though not without some reluctance, but even so, I'm not breathing any easier. Despite being harassed all night by a mystery man in a balaclava brandishing multiple weapons, there seems to be something even scarier about this other guy. Maybe it's the way he's so calm and oozes confidence despite this being a tense situation.

How do I know he's confident?

He's not wearing a mask over his face.

The man looks to be in his sixties and has a healthy tan to go with his smart haircut. His hair might be grey but it's clearly been styled, and he is wearing a trendy winter coat that gives him more of a youthful appearance. But I don't care what he looks like. I just care about who he is.

'It's you, isn't it?' I ask him, trying to inject a little confidence of my own into my voice. 'You're the one who's doing all this to me. You're paying him. And you were watching me on camera.'

'That's right,' the man says.

'What kind of freak has a prison cell built to keep people in?' I scream at him, hoping to offend him a little with the name-calling.

But it doesn't work.

'The kind of freak who used to own this house,' he replies before taking a seat on the sofa opposite me.

40

It takes me a moment to comprehend what he has just said. But when I do, there is only one thing I can say.

'Franz?'

The German nods his head before putting one arm across the back of the sofa, looking extremely comfortable as if he's making himself at home. But this is not his home anymore. It's mine. He sold this house to me, or at least the estate agent who he put in charge of completing the sale did. I never actually met the homeowner at any point, only hearing titbits of information from the middleman between us. But I did get his name, and I also knew that he was German, so I've put two and two together here, and it seems like I've come up with the right answer.

The previous owner, the man who built this house, and the one who I bought it from, is the one who has been trying to kill me.

'You're the one behind this?' I say, confused and angry. 'You've been the one putting me through all of this tonight? But why?'

'Oh, I have my reasons, and we'll get to those in a moment. First of all, would you go and check on my wife and make sure she is okay?'

That question was directed at the man in the balaclava and like the obedient servant he is, he does as he is told, leaving the room to go back outside the house but not before he has handed the gun to the German.

'Your wife?' I ask.

'Yes, she was the one driving the car that you got into earlier. Quite a coincidence, don't you think?'

He laughs then, but it's a strange laugh. Just one of the many strange things about this man.

'Of course, it wasn't a coincidence. I had her out there on the road in her car just in case you managed to escape tonight. All she had to do was stop and let you in, and she could bring you straight back here. I'm sorry if she got your hopes up and made you think that she was going to take you some place safe.'

I think about the woman in the car and how she easily let me inside and started driving without asking any questions. Come to think of it, she didn't say anything at all.

'If my wife was quiet with you, then I want you to know that it's nothing personal,' Franz goes on. 'She just didn't want you to hear her German accent and have you figure all of this out before I had a chance to speak to you first.'

'Figure all of this out?' I hiss back, shocked he could even suggest I might have any clue what is going on here. 'I don't know why somebody would do this to me, never mind you! So tell me!'

'Don't worry, I will. Just calm down.'

Telling a frustrated person to calm down is never a good strategy, and I let him know it.

'Calm down? You've been trying to kill me! You killed Damian and Charlie! And you probably killed my neighbours! Not to mention you have some weird cell underneath this house that I had absolutely no idea about! How the hell can you expect me to calm down after all of that?'

'I admit that it won't be easy,' Franz says, removing his arm from the back of the sofa and resting his hands on his lap, still very much looking like a man who has called around for a cup of tea and a chat about what's been in the news recently rather than the mastermind behind a devious plot.

'Easy? You're a psycho! And that guy you've paid to do this, the one in the balaclava? He's even more of a psycho than you!'

'It's not a competition,' Franz says before showcasing that awful laugh of his again. 'He was just doing his job. But I can take it from here.'

'Take what from here? Why the hell are you doing this to me?'

'What's the matter? You don't seem to appreciate the man who built this house from the ground up stopping by to see how things are going. I don't think that's very hospitable of you. After all, without me, you wouldn't have this wonderful home to call your own now.'

It is a beautiful home, or at least I thought it was before it became tainted by everything that has happened tonight. And by the realisation that there was some weird underground dungeon in it too.

'But why are you punishing me?' I ask, exhausted to have to keep asking. 'You put the house up for sale, and you accepted my offer to buy it!'

'Ahhh yes, your offer. I remember that,' Franz says with a small shake of the head. 'It was the offer that wasn't as high as I would have liked it to have been.'

'You're mad at me because I didn't pay the full asking price? Is that it?'

'Not quite.'

'I was entitled to negotiate, just like you were!'

'Except you didn't negotiate, did you?'

I pause there as I recall the bidding process I was involved in to get this house.

'From what I remember,' Franz goes on. 'It was less of a negotiation and more of an ultimatum.'

I say nothing to that.

'You gave your final offer and then said it was take it or leave it, isn't that right?'

'But you could have left it if you didn't like it. You didn't have to accept it!'

'You were told my reasons for selling, right?'

I nod my head. 'Your wife was ill.'

'She still is.'

'She seems alright to me.'

I perhaps shouldn't have said that, but I'm angry.

'That hat she is wearing covers up a giant scar on the top of her head,' Franz tells me. 'The head that was shaven just before she underwent a gruelling twelve-hour operation.'

'That sounds awful, but how was I supposed to know that?'

'The estate agent told you my wife was ill, yes?'

'Yes, but that didn't have anything to do with me or the offer I made you.'

'Why are you lying to me?'

'I'm not!'

Franz tuts before reaching into his pocket. But just in case I have any ideas about trying to make a run for the door while he's distracted, he raises the head of the gun in my direction to let me know it's still something I have to worry about.

'I have something for you to listen to,' Franz says as he takes his phone out. 'But before you do, I need to check the time.'

He makes a point of doing so before tapping on his phone screen.

'What are you doing?' I ask him, growing impatient.

'I'm just letting you know how long you've got left,' he says as he types.

'We're not still doing this, are we?' I retort. 'What is it with you guys and this damn hour?'

'Oh, it's very important, actually,' Franz tells me before turning his screen around for me to see what's on it.

More numbers. And they're descending, of course.

But they're not as big as they used to be.

This timer says I only have ten minutes left.

41

Great. The timer is back again. Not only that, but there's not much time left on it now. But this little trick of showing me how many minutes I have left to live is wearing thin, and to prove that point, I just roll my eyes at Franz.

'Not this again. You know what I think? I think this is all one big bluff, and you aren't going to actually kill me. You'd have done it already. But you don't have the balls. Not you and not that guy in the balaclava. So you might as well go ahead and make that timer show zero. It doesn't make a difference. I'm not afraid of you or anybody else.'

I might be exaggerating, but I hope that worked. If it has, then maybe Franz will stop wasting his time and leave before he makes this worse for himself. If he has any sense, then he could be on a plane out of the country before the police catch up with him.

But he doesn't seem too bothered about getting caught as he taps away on his phone and when he's ready, he holds it up so I can hear the audio recording he's just started playing.

'Greg? It's Katherine. What's going on? I've been trying to reach you all afternoon. What kind of estate agent doesn't answer their phone? Look, I'm sick of waiting for Franz to make his mind up about selling to me or not, so here's my final offer. 1.3 million. Take it or leave it. I know it's below the asking price, but I also know that his wife is desperately ill, and they are eager to return to Germany before she gets any worse. So he *doesn't really have time to negotiate anymore, does he? So give him my offer and tell him he has one hour to say yes or no. One hour. Or I'm walking away, and good luck to him finding another cash buyer in this market.'*

The recording finishes then, and Franz puts his phone down, so I'm able to see the timer again.

'That was your voice on the recording, yes?' he asks me, but we both know it was, so there's no need for me to confirm it.

'That was a message that you left on the answer phone of the estate agent when this house was on the market, and you were trying to buy it.'

'I know what it is,' I say without making eye contact.

'Good. How do you feel hearing it back?'

I say nothing.

'Shame? Regret? Disgust?'

All the words Franz suggests might be indicative of how I'm feeling inside but I don't want to give him the pleasure of knowing that, so I just shake my head.

'So all of this is about the damn house?' I ask him. 'This pile of bricks has caused all of this?'

'No, this is all about the way you treat people and how you seem to think that your way is the only way in life.'

'I was trying to buy a house! I made an offer with a deadline! That's good business sense! What did you want me to do? Say that I had an unlimited budget and was under no pressure to find a home, so I was open to negotiating for months and months and paying whatever price you wanted me to? That's ludicrous!'

189

'There's showing good business sense and then there's showing a little humanity,' Franz snarls back at me, the first time he has lost his cool with me. 'You used the fact that my wife was ill to gain leverage and pressure me into a quick sale for a price that was less than this home was worth!'

'You could have said no! You didn't have to accept my offer!'

'But you knew I was compromised! You knew I wanted to get my wife back to Germany and you used that against me! What kind of a person does that? And you knew how much this house meant to me. I made sure the estate agent impressed on you how I poured my life and soul into this place, only to have to sell it when fate conspired against me and my family. Yet you still couldn't show a little heart and pay the measly extra £100k just to meet the asking price. I know you could afford it, but you had to win, didn't you? You had to get what you wanted once again, and to hell with everybody else. You know, that extra hundred thousand pounds would have been nothing to you, but to me and my family, it made the difference in the care we were able to get for my wife.'

I'm shocked by the pure anger and passion that erupts from Franz after previously seeing him as a cool character who didn't look like he could be ruffled by anything. It's also clear that this is an anger and a passion that he has been holding in for a long time, which explains why he has gone to such lengths to make my life a living hell tonight.

But does it justify them? The threats. The violence? The sheer audacity of it all?

Of course not.

'Okay, so I might have done some things I'm not proud of, and I could have shown a little more heart to you and your family.'

'And what about all the other people you did this to? Your ex-boyfriend. The clients. Your brother.'

'You're right! I'm not proud of any of it! But what can I do? Like I said before, I can't change the past.'

'But you can die for your sins,' Franz says, the calm demeanour back and just at the worst possible time. Telling me he wants to kill me when he's angry is one thing but it's even more chilling when he does it calmly.

'Just like you've done to so many people, you've been given an hour, an arbitrary amount of time but one that you clearly have no problem giving people. What I want to know is how did it feel? Uncomfortable? Like you were under pressure? Like you were having to do something you didn't want to do? Well, congratulations, now you know exactly how Damian, Charlie and Laura felt. And now you know how I felt too.'

Franz actually looks relieved to have got all of that off his chest, as if he's been practising that speech for a while. He probably has. All of this certainly took some planning. But not all of it. Some things had to have been planned before.

Before me.

Like the cell under the house.

'Who are you?' I ask Franz, surprising him with my question because he raises his eyebrows as if he wasn't expecting me to turn this back on him.

'Excuse me?'

'We all know exactly who I am now. The things I've said. The things I'm capable of. The mistakes I've made. But what about you? What are you hiding? What mistakes have you made in the past?'

'This isn't about me.'

'Okay,' I reply. 'Then let's not talk about you. Let's talk about Karl instead. Who was he? And why was he trapped in that room under this house before I even got here?'

42

'How do you know about Karl?' Franz asks me, clearly taken aback at the mention of the name.

'I'm guessing you didn't spend too much time looking around that cell of yours before you moved out,' I reply, glad to finally have the upper hand on at least one thing. 'The name was written on the wall. Or should I say, scratched into the wall.'

Franz still looks unsure, but I'll keep pressing him on this subject because, with less than eight minutes left on the timer, it might be the only possible thing I could distract him with now and hopefully buy myself some more time.

'I guess you didn't look hard enough before you left that cell and sealed it off from me,' I say. 'That is what you did, isn't it? I wasn't supposed to find that underground room, and I never would have if you hadn't come back to do this to me.'

Franz gets to his feet then and walks over to the window, not answering me before he carefully peels back a portion of the curtain and looks outside.

'Who is Karl?' I ask again. 'Or should I say, who was he? I'm guessing he's dead.'

'It doesn't concern you,' Franz tells me, still peeping through the curtains, and I think about making a run for it, but he still has the gun in his hand, and I don't particularly fancy getting shot in the back as I lunge for the door.

'Why can't you tell me? What difference would it make if you're going to kill me soon? It's not as if I can pass his name onto the police.'

'Because it's none of your business.'

Franz moves away from the curtain and heads back towards the sofa but before he passes me, he fixes me with a deadly stare.

'My wife is going to come inside now and join us for a moment, but you will not mention Karl in front of her,' he tells me. 'If you do, then I will take five minutes off this timer and considering how little is left on it anyway, that won't leave you with much time at all.'

Franz goes to the door and awaits his wife while I consider the threat he just made. It would obviously be a very bad thing for me to do to lose five minutes when I already have less than eight left. But he clearly doesn't want me to mention Karl in front of his wife.

I wonder why?

I watch as he greets his wife in the doorway and guides her into the room, his hand on her arm as he helps her to the sofa. She looks a little tired, although not tired enough to have picked me up in her car outside and driven me back here. But Franz is clearly concerned about her and is making sure she is comfortable, and only once she is sitting down does he let go of her.

She keeps her eyes on me while her husband returns to the door and whispers something to the man in the balaclava, who doesn't come inside the room himself but lingers in the doorway, possibly blocking my one and only escape route should I try to run in my last few minutes. But I'm not thinking about running again. I'm thinking about why Franz doesn't want me to mention Karl's name in front of his wife.

The woman sitting opposite me is pale and gaunt and definitely looks like somebody who has been battling ill health. But there's a steeliness behind her eyes when she looks at me, and I guess she is as happy about this revenge mission as her husband is.

Damn, they must really hate me. Then again, I did come across poorly in that voicemail message.

'Let's make this quick because we don't have any other choice,' Franz says, stepping back into the room. 'You're almost out of time, Katherine, so it's now or never. You wouldn't apologise to me but perhaps you would like to apologise to my wife, Greta. As you can see, she's still very much recovering from the ordeal she has been through with her health. The doctors. The operations. The constant stress. And while all that was going on, she had to listen to a voicemail message from you, in which you clearly had no compassion for her or what either of us were going through. How does that make you feel as you sit here across from her today and look her in the eyes?'

It does make me feel bad, but my shame is tempered somewhat by what this couple has done to me in return, and I'm not sure I'd call us even. But for the sake of trying something different, because nothing else has worked for me so far, I consider apologising to see what difference that might make.

'I'm sorry,' I say, shaking my head to show just how much I'm ashamed of my past behaviour. 'I should have been nicer and more considerate of what you were going through. You didn't deserve me making demands when you were already suffering. I could have made the whole process much easier for you instead of being a bitch. I see that now.'

Franz genuinely looks surprised at what I've said, as does Greta. But do they accept my apology? And will it have any impact on what they do to me next?

I wait to see what their reaction will be, and they share a glance before Franz speaks again.

'Well, that's something, I suppose. Better late than never. But it doesn't change anything. All that is going to happen now is my wife and I will leave here, and our friend in the balaclava will deal with you. Then this matter will be over. I suspect it won't be long until this house is on the market again, and who knows, maybe I'll buy it back. Then again, there are a few bad memories here now, so perhaps not.'

Franz smiles at me before holding out his hand for his wife to take. She wearily gets up from the sofa and starts to make her way to the door. As they go, I see there are just a little over six minutes left on the timer. This really wouldn't be a good point for me to do something stupid, something like lose five minutes off that clock by mentioning a certain person's name.

But to hell with it, what have I got to lose now?

'I know about Karl,' I say to Greta, causing her to stop walking away from me. 'What I don't know is why your husband didn't want me to mention him in front of you. Maybe it has something to do with the fact that he was put in a prison cell underneath this house.'

196

Franz freezes as his face goes red and his eyes bore into me. But it's too late now. Sure, I might have just lost five minutes and be dead in sixty seconds. But judging by the look on Greta's face, I might also have just caused her to no longer be on her partner's side.

43

'Kill her,' Franz tells the man in the balaclava as he tries to bundle Greta out of the room and clear space for me to meet my demise. But Greta is not going easily. She wants to know why I just said what I did.

'What are you talking about?' she asks me, ignoring her husband's insistence that she leave quickly. 'What do you mean there is a prison cell underneath this house? And what has it got to do with Karl?'

'Ignore her, she's just trying to distract us and save herself, but it won't work,' Franz cries. 'Her time is up. Goodbye, Katherine.'

He seems to think that he can get Greta to leave now, and as the man in the balaclava steps towards me, I fear it really might be the end. But Greta fights back, showing strength that her diminutive and weak stature belies, and what she says next explains why she suddenly found a reason to be stronger.

'What do you know about my son?' she asks me, pushing away her husband and trying to make eye contact with me around the man who is still approaching me.

Now I know who Karl is.

He's Franz and Greta's child.

'I know he was locked away in that cell,' I scream, leaping away from my sofa before the man in the balaclava can put his hands on me. Franz still has the gun, but the man nearest to me has a knife, and I see the light reflecting off the blade as he raises it in my direction.

'What cell? Franz, what is she talking about?'

Greta wants the truth, clearly knowing nothing about the underground prison I was kept in but that also must have housed her son at one point if his name was scratched into the wall.

'We're leaving!' Franz says, dragging his wife from the room, and as they disappear from view, I realise I'm backed into the corner of the room as far as I can possibly be from the door, and there's no way for me to get past the man with the knife.

This is it.

He's not going to let me get away again.

Franz has left his phone on the table, no doubt expecting the man in the balaclava to pick it up for him in a moment when he's finished with me. But because it's here, I can see the timer on the screen, and I see that I still have five minutes left. But it's little consolation because I don't expect the man brandishing the knife to honour it, and sure enough, he has no intention of doing so as he raises the knife above my head and prepares to bring it down onto me.

I close my eyes and wait for the pain.

But all I hear is a gunshot.

44

I open my eyes and when I do, I see the knife has been lowered, and the man in the mask is looking away from me and in the direction of the doorway. The sound of the gunshot came from the hallway, just where Franz and Greta were leaving.

But what just happened?

And why is Greta screaming?

'Franz?' the man standing in front of me says, calling out to see what his boss is doing. But there's no response. All we can hear is Greta, who is still very distressed.

But then I hear whispering. Somebody is talking to her.

But who?

I don't take the risk of waiting to find out and instead choose to make my last-ditch bid for freedom, pushing the man with the knife away from me and sending him hurtling backwards over the coffee table. As he groans and loses grip of the knife, I rush for the doorway, and I'm planning on not stopping for anything or anybody.

And then I see who is standing in the hallway with the gun in one hand and a dead Franz lying by his feet.

My brother.

'Oli, what are you doing here?' I cry, stunned.

'Are you okay? Did they hurt you?' he asks me, eyeing me up and down for any signs of visible injuries.

'Why are you here?' I ask him, ignoring his question as I try to get my head around his sudden appearance in my house. I haven't seen him since the day he told me he hated me and blamed me for his wife's death, but boy, am I glad he seems to have changed his mind about that because he's just saved my life.

Or is he still too late?

The man in the balaclava rushes at me then, pushing me to the floor as he makes his own bid to get away, and as he runs towards the kitchen and the open back door, Oli fires another gunshot, this one in his direction.

The sound is deafening, and I put my hands to my ears as I lie on the floor and try to avoid the bullets. But the man trying to get away manages to avoid them too, and as another shot is fired, I'm dismayed to see that my brother seems to have missed both times. The man flees into the kitchen, where Oli goes to give chase.

'No, leave him!' I cry, grabbing my brother's leg and stopping him from following. 'It's too dangerous!'

Now that he's unexpectedly come back into my life, I'd hate for something to happen to him, so I cling on to his leg and while he tries to break free, I simply don't let go. Sure, it means the man who almost stabbed me is going to get away, but I can't risk my brother losing his life, not over me and especially not after what he's already lost where I was concerned.

'He's getting away!' Oli cries, angry at me for halting his progress.

'I don't care,' I tell him, and when he looks down at me, he sees that I mean it. I'm crying now because not only does it feel like this ordeal might finally be over, but I have my sibling back, and I don't want to lose him again.

'What are you doing here? Why did you come?' I ask him, forever grateful that he did but confused as to why he changed his mind about me.

'You sent me that message earlier,' he says, referring to the text in which I said I was thinking about him. The text that he didn't respond to.

It's only then, as things calm down slightly, that I notice Greta sitting on the floor by the front door and holding onto the hand of her dead husband.

But she is not crying like I am.

She is looking at me.

'My son went missing when he was six,' she says, her voice low and her hand still holding Franz's. 'Just before my husband finished construction on this house and we moved in. He disappeared. We thought he was taken, and the police eventually thought so too, but there was no evidence, and he was never found. I've gone all these years, never knowing what happened to him. Almost trying to forget about him because it hurt too much when he came to mind. Do you have any idea what it feels like to try and forget the name of your child? But I did. I'd pushed it from my memory. Until you said his name today.'

She lets go of her husband's hand then and gets to her feet. I figure I should try and do the same, and as Oli helps me up, I know what I have to do.

'I can show you where your husband kept me,' I say, knowing Greta had no idea about the underground room based on how surprised she was when I mentioned it earlier.

'We need to get you out of here,' Oli tells me, but I'm going to show Greta what she needs to see, and he isn't stopping me.

It's funny, but despite this woman being involved in the plot to kill me tonight, everything changed when I realised Franz was keeping a secret from her. And seeing the way he manhandled her out of the living room when she was trying to ask me a question about Karl suggested the German man was accustomed to getting his wife to do whatever he wanted her to do.

So despite it all, Greta might just be a victim in this like I am. And the fact she doesn't seem as distraught about the death of her husband as one might expect her to be only lends credence to the idea that she might not have been entirely happy with Franz and the things he made her do.

I lead her back to the hatch that takes us onto the staircase down into the corridor. From there, it's just a short walk to the iron door, and after asking Oli to turn the torchlight on on his phone so we can see better down here, we enter the cell from which I was lucky to escape from earlier.

I see the broken bulb and the cable, but it's the marking on the wall that I'm really looking for, and while it takes me a moment, I find it. When I do, I point it out to Greta, who drops to her knees to get a closer look.

She stares at the name on the wall for a moment before rubbing a hand over its rough edges. When she does, she starts crying, the kind of crying I would have expected her to do after her husband got shot.

This is real emotion, pure and powerful.

The love of a mother.

A mother who might finally have found out what happened to her lost son.

45

'He was a difficult child,' Greta says as she remains by the marking on the wall, possibly the last mark her young son ever made in this world. 'A lot of behavioural problems. Not like his older brother and sister. Franz said they were no trouble. But he struggled with Karl. Never got as close to him as he did the other two. Maybe that was my fault. He never wanted a third child. But I got pregnant, and when we had him, I figured everything would be okay. But it wasn't. Karl's upbringing was difficult. And it got even harder when I fell sick.'

I share a look with Oli, who is standing behind Greta, holding the torchlight so we can all see each other down here. He looks uncomfortable, as he well might, because he knows we shouldn't be wasting time doing this. We should be talking to the police and dealing with the dead body upstairs, as well as making sure that man in the balaclava is being hunted down. But I want to hear what Greta has to say or answer her if she has any more questions for me because it's clear she is a broken woman, and the piece of her that is missing has nothing to do with her husband and everything to do with her son.

'Franz must have built this room as a place he could hide Karl,' Greta goes on, piecing it together in her mind, which is the only option available to her now he is dead. 'That explains why he went missing not long after construction on the house was finished. He must have been put down here. But for how long?'

Greta sobs loudly then, tormenting herself with the idea of her little boy being left down here for a long time. I have no idea how much time he did spend down here, but if he was never seen again, then it obviously only ended in one way.

'How could you do this?' Greta screams. 'How could you hurt our son, you evil bastard?'

Franz is not around to hear and answer those answers, nor will he be around to answer for his crimes, those concerning Karl and those related to me. But at least he can't do anything else now.

'I'm sorry,' I say, deeply meaning it. 'But we need to call the police and let them look into all of this.'

Greta pulls herself together then, no doubt sobered by the thought of uniformed officers swarming this house and asking a lot of difficult questions about her and her family.

'What are you going to say to them about me?' she wants to know, meekly looking up at me from where she kneels on the ground.

I'm not too sure, so I hesitate and as I do, Greta makes her case for forgiveness.

'It was Franz's idea, I swear!' she tells me desperately. 'He wanted to do this to you. He was the one who bore a grudge. I told him to leave it and move on, but he couldn't forget you. He was a man who was used to getting his own way, so he didn't like it when you gave him the ultimatum about the house. And he definitely didn't like it when the estate agent advised him to accept your offer within the stated timeframe.'

'I was just negotiating,' I say, repeating the same argument I made to Franz upstairs earlier.

'I know that,' Greta says with a shake of the head. 'And any other sensible person would have known that too. But my husband was not a rational man. He didn't make the money required to build a home like this by being rational. He built it by following his emotions and acting instinctively. But for some reason, he changed the habit of a lifetime when it came to you and the house, and he accepted the offer. I guess my illness was a distraction for him. But it ate away at him that you got your way and paid less than he originally wanted. That was why he came back to England once my prognosis was a little better. It was why he followed you and tried to find out as much about you as he could.'

'He followed me?'

Greta nods. 'He watched you here. Of course, he knew where you lived, didn't he? And he followed you. To work. To the gym. To any meetings you had with other people, be it personal or professional. And he stalked you online. Looked up old contacts. Asked around. Tried to find out if you had any enemies. Well, besides him, of course.'

'Your husband was crazy,' I say, stating the obvious, and Greta doesn't disagree with me.

'I'll admit he did not behave normally,' she says. 'But I only knew most of what he was doing when he came back to Germany and told me. When he returned, he had a look in his eye. It was the same look he used to get whenever he felt he was on the verge of a successful business deal or even when we were younger, and I promised him myself that night in our bedroom. It was the look that said he knew he was going to get what he wanted. And what he wanted was revenge.'

'No, what he did was worse than that,' I tell Greta, surprised that I have to be the one to keep telling her just what her husband was really like. 'Revenge on me for a perceived slight is one thing. But he went beyond that. He killed innocent people. My ex-boyfriend and one of my clients. What had they ever done to him? And that man he hired, the one in the balaclava, he might have killed my neighbours. So whatever Franz said he was going to do - what he actually did was much worse.'

'I know that,' Greta says, her head bowed now. 'And I'm deeply ashamed to have been involved with it. But he was a very persuasive man. He made me help him. I had no choice; you have to believe me!'

Greta is clearly afraid of the prospect of prison, as well she might be. But does she really deserve it? Not if she was forced into helping her evil husband, and if tonight has taught us one thing, her husband truly was an evil man.

'I have two other children,' Greta reminds me. 'They'll have nothing if I go to prison. They've already lost their little brother, and now their father is dead. He deserves to have died, but I have to look after them. Please, can you forgive me? I beg you.'

I can see that Greta means her apology, and when I look at Oli, he seems to have got the same vibe. He subtly nods his head at me as if to say that Greta's involvement in this should be kept from the police.

And I'm inclined to agree.

'Okay,' I say to Greta, granting her wish whilst showing possibly superhuman levels of forgiveness. 'I'll tell them it was all Franz. But enough is enough. We need to call the police, and we need to call them now.'

46

If it was daunting to see my home infiltrated by a masked man with a knife, then it was almost just as daunting to see it swarming with police officers, their marked cars having been parked on my driveway and their uniformed bodies quickly bustling around my house.

They asked questions when they arrived, they looked for evidence and most of all, they tried to piece together exactly what went on here on what should have just been a typical Friday night in this quiet town.

But while it might have been a little hard to believe everything I was saying when they first got here, things soon became more understandable for them once they had a chance to investigate what I had told them and seen several things with their own eyes.

Like my car with the flat tyres on the drive, which had made it impossible for me to get away quickly when I escaped. Like the broken chair in the dining room that I had once been tied to. Like the bullet holes in the kitchen door where my brother had fired at the man in the balaclava as he became the one who ran. Like the underground prison cell that would not show up on any official plans for this property and was definitely not the kind of thing any innocent homeowner would ever construct in their house. And most of all, like the discovery that awaited the police officers after I had sent them next door to check on my neighbours.

I had feared that Fred and Norma, along with Rosie, the nurse, were already dead, so imagine my surprise when I was told that they had been found alive, extremely shaken by their ordeal but otherwise well. All three of them had been tied up, so they had been unable to escape, but at least they were okay.

I was informed that all three of them had been taken to hospital and would remain there for observation for a while, which also gave me a little time to figure out what I was going to do about the fact that I had caught Rosie and Fred trying to kill Norma. But that was a problem that would have to wait for a little while because before I could even think about that, I had several questions to answer.

'Talk me through exactly what happened.'

'What time did you receive the letter through your door?'

'Did you take it seriously, or did you think it was a prank?'

'You have no idea who the man in the balaclava could have been?'

'Do you have addresses for Damian and Charlie so we can check on them?'

'What exactly happened at your neighbours' house?'

'Walk me through exactly how you escaped the cell again.'

'You say Franz did all this because of how you treated him during the sale?'

'What time did your brother arrive at the house?'

'So you didn't see Franz get shot yourself?'

'Why did you stop your brother going after the man in the balaclava if you knew he was going to get away?'

And last but not least, *'You're saying Greta had nothing to do with any of this? If not, why was she here?'*

It was a whole barrage of questions and statements, and there was a lot to talk about. But despite knowing I needed to explain myself clearly to the police so they knew the full story, there was only one person I actually wanted to talk to, and that was my brother, who had saved my life.

I was told that Oli was being questioned in another room, as was Greta, and our stories were being corroborated and our sentences sifted through to make sure that what they were saying added up, and there were no loose ends or inaccuracies. Hopefully, they don't find any reason to poke holes in our version of events and, ultimately, allow the three of us to walk free. But any incident that involves a dead body greeting the officers when they arrive at a house is always going to be investigated thoroughly, so I had no choice but to keep answering the questions and hoping they believed me.

Much like the arrival of the police was a relief to me, it was a relief to see them go, satisfied with the story I had given them, for now anyway, and they were also allowing Oli and Greta to go too. But we had to stay contactable at all times, which we assured them we would, and when they asked where they could find me, I was thrilled to hear Oli say that I was welcome to stay with him while my house was still being dissected by the law.

I was grateful for the offer, not just because I didn't fancy going back to my home so quickly after what had happened, but also because it boded well for my future relationship with my brother.

As I arrived at his property, a place I hadn't been for such a long time, I was instantly reminded of what this house had been missing. It wasn't my presence but that of Laura, Oli's faithful wife, as well as the presence of a little boy who would have no doubt filled this home with the sounds of laughter and mischief. But the only sign of them in this house now was the photo of Laura, on the mantelpiece, a picture of her cradling her bump, an image that was captured just a few weeks before her accident.

I felt like suggesting to my brother that having the photo on view on the mantelpiece for him to look at every day possibly wasn't the best way for him to get over what happened, but I kept my thoughts to myself. Just like I didn't mention that the best thing for him to do might be to sell up and move somewhere else so he can have a fresh start away from the memories of the woman he lost.

The last thing I wanted to do was make him angry or upset, not only because he had just saved my life but because he had just come back into it, and I wanted him to stay in it now he was back. That was why I said very little for the first half an hour we were alone together, choosing instead to listen to everything Oli had to say, allowing him to get things off his chest that had clearly been on it for a while.

'It was wrong of me to blame you for what happened with Laura,' he said after he had spent a little time dancing around the point with small talk. 'I know you weren't to blame for the accident. You weren't to know that a lorry driver was going to hit her. Besides, such a thing could have happened anytime, when she was on her way to a maternity class or driving home from the supermarket. Traffic accidents happen every day. Maybe it was fate. Whatever it was, nothing will bring her back now, and I need to accept that.'

I had wept as my brother had forgiven me, and even though I didn't completely absolve myself of all responsibility like he was doing for me, I was glad he no longer hated me because losing Laura was one thing, but losing his sibling as well was just another unnecessary tragedy, for him and for me.

After much weeping from the pair of us, as well as several tight hugs, we were able to move on from the distant past and discuss more recent events, namely his arrival at my house just when I needed him most.

'You sent me that text message earlier in the day,' Oli reminded me.

'That was why you came?'

'I'd been thinking about contacting you again for some time. But I don't know if I was brave enough to make the first move. But after reading your message and re-reading all the older ones you sent me, I knew you were hurting as much as I was, so I plucked up the courage, and I came to your house. But obviously, I wasn't expecting to walk in on what I did.'

Oli told me about how he arrived to find the driveway gate open and noticed the front door to the house was open too. After noting my flat tyres when he passed my car, he entered the home, and that was when he saw Franz dragging Greta to the door with a gun in his hand. Figuring something was terribly wrong, Oli engaged with Franz, trying to free the stricken woman, and in the struggle, as he fought for his life, Oli was able to turn the gun on the German man and kill him before he could pull the trigger instead.

His misfortune at turning up at the wrong place at the wrong time was my good luck because I have no doubt that I wouldn't be here now if it wasn't for him. But I am, and as he goes to answer a knock at his front door, I relax deeper into his sofa, my hands warmed by the hot mug of tea that my sibling made me and my head filled with all sorts of nice thoughts about what my brother and I can do together in the future now we're back on speaking terms.

But when he answers the door, I hear voices in the hallway, and it sounds like the police are back.

I let out a deep sigh, hating that mine and Oli's reunion of sorts is now going to be interrupted by yet more questions from those in uniform. But before they enter the living room, I receive a text message on my phone, the one that was returned to me after the police had found it hidden in my house and checked it to make sure there was nothing incriminating on there.

The message is a simple one.

Hey, I just heard the news. Are you okay?

But there's nothing simple about the person who sent it.

That's because it's from Damian, my ex-boyfriend.

The one who should be dead.

47

It was only one minute after I received the message from Damian that a police officer confirmed the confusing state of affairs. My ex-boyfriend was alive, despite me being told otherwise, and he wasn't the only one.

Charlie, my former client, was alive too.

The police had visited both men after I had informed them about the photos I had been shown by the man in the balaclava, the ones in which it appeared both Damian and Charlie had been murdered. Expecting to make grim discoveries at the two properties, the officers had been surprised to find the two men well, albeit very shocked and confused as to why the police were at their door. Now the man who has just told me about all of that is asking me why I was so convinced they were dead.

'I saw the photos!' I cry.

'Photos of Damian and Charlie?'

'Yes!'

'And you could see their faces clearly in the images?'

'Yes, I could!'

'And these photos were on the phone of the man in the balaclava?'

'That's right! Have you found him yet?'

'As my colleagues discussed with you earlier, without much of a description to go on, it is going to be very difficult to track him down.'

'But you have to! He might come back for me!'

'This house is being watched day and night, and I assure you that you're safe. What we need to ascertain right now is how and why you believe you were shown photos of two deceased men from your past who were not actually dead.'

'I guess he was just trying to scare me,' I say. 'That must be it. He figured showing me such a thing would make me take him more seriously, and it sure as hell worked.'

'But what I'm getting at is if you were shown photos of Damian and Charlie, then they must have been staged.'

I suddenly realise that he is right. If those two men are not dead, those photos were faked.

But they were still in them.

'Oh my God, are they involved in this too?' I cry, horrified at the thought. 'Were they helping the man in the balaclava?'

For the first time since this ordeal ended, I can feel all the old symptoms of fear coming back. The tight chest. The racing heart. I thought this was all over. But now it seems like there might be more to this nightmare.

'We have interviewed both men but neither of them has said anything that makes us think they were involved in this plot against you,' the police officer tells me.

'And you believe them?' Oli chips in, one of his hands on my shoulder, which makes me feel nice, like when he used to look after me when we were younger.

'Without being able to see the images in question for ourselves, it's very difficult for us to know exactly what they contain and whether or not the two men might be involved.'

'But I told you what they contain,' I cry, struggling to control the volume of my voice. 'And they must be involved. If not, then they would be dead, right?'

'Again, it's very difficult without any actual evidence.'

'Why don't you believe me? You think I'm making it up?'

Oli squeezes my shoulder, no doubt as a subtle way to tell me to keep calm, but I can't. Not if Damian and Charlie were involved in this too. But how can I prove it?

'I'm not safe,' I say, realising this is far from over. 'Franz was just one of the people who wanted me dead. But the rest of them are still out there. Damian. Charlie. The man in the balaclava. And you're telling me you're not going to arrest Damian and Charlie, nor can you find the man in the balaclava? So what does that mean? You're not going to have police officers watching over me forever, are you? At some point, you're going to leave me, and then what? I'll just be a sitting duck stuck in my house, waiting for them to come back and have another go at me.'

'No, that is not the case,' the police officer says, but he's not convincing, and the way he glances at the doorway just after he speaks says volumes about how he wants this awkward conversation to be over now.

'Talk to Greta again,' I suggest. 'She might know something about Damian and Charlie that could help.'

'We have done, but she claims to have not known anything about them.'

This feels like a good time to tell the police that Greta was initially involved in the plot against me and helped her husband recapture me but to do so would mean changing my story, and that would only get me in trouble. Besides, poor Greta has been through plenty, what with her abusive husband and lost son to consider. But what am I supposed to do if the police aren't taking this as seriously as I am?

What am I supposed to do if this is never actually over?

48

It's been one week since my life was almost taken by a sinister plot against me and in all that time, I've barely slept a wink. How can I when I'm still worrying that there are people out there who wish me dead?

Having spent many a restless night thinking about it, I have come to the conclusion that I regret not letting Oli go after the man in the balaclava. I was worried for my brother's safety, but maybe if I had let him go, then he could have shot that man, and he would have been one less thing to worry about. But he got away, and now, as the police keep reminding me, without me being able to provide a physical description of his facial features, it's going to be almost impossible to figure out who it was.

It's not difficult to picture that balaclava every time I close my eyes to try and get some rest. It haunts me, or rather the eyes behind the mask haunt me. There's a man out there walking around who shouldn't be. He's free, unlike I am, trapped in my brother's house, watched over by police officers and too scared to go back to my own house for five minutes just to grab a few items.

This is no way for me to live, but what else can I do? Go home and risk him coming back for me? Or just keep praying that the police will make a lucky breakthrough?

What is almost as concerning as all of that is thinking about Damian and Charlie and how they must have been involved in this plot as well. Yet they are walking free too. Is anybody going to pay for this crime?

Sure, Franz might have paid with his life, but he was just the ringleader. He had accomplices, and all of them got off scot-free. I might have given Greta the opportunity to get away with it but only because there were extenuating circumstances there.

But I sure as hell don't want any of the others to get away with it.

I have considered texting Damian and pretending to not be aware he might be involved, playing the worried ex-girlfriend and seeing what information I might be able to extract from him. But he already knows that I thought he was dead because I sent the police to his place, so if he is involved, he will know that I'm merely trying to bait him into making a mistake. The same goes for Charlie too.

So what can I do other than hope they slip up and implicate themselves?

Charlie and Damian must have been shocked to learn about me surviving, as well as hearing that Franz died. That was clearly not how things were supposed to go. I wonder if they all planned to meet up after the event and celebrate my demise together. Perhaps raise a glass to the death of the woman they hated for various reasons. But their plan was scuppered, and now they must be wondering if they're going to get away with it.

But it's today while sitting in Oli's house alone while he is back at work, with a police officer in a car outside the property keeping watch on all comings and goings, that I wonder if Damian and Charlie might have been manipulated into going along with Franz's plan by the German man himself. After all, it was Franz who came up with the idea, and I saw how he clearly manipulated his wife into helping him, so why not others too? What if Damian and Charlie were threatened and/or blackmailed into posing for those photos in which it looked like they were dead? If so, maybe they are innocent, and it might just explain why Damian messaged me last week to ask if I was okay.

I walk over to the window and check outside to see if the officer in the car is still there and of course he is. He's currently tucking into a packaged sandwich, no doubt bored at being assigned here. While remaining by the window, I call Damian, wondering if he will pick up. Either he really does hate my guts, in which case he might not answer for fear of incriminating himself, or he is innocent but might hate me for thinking he is involved. Either way, the odds of him answering are low, plus it's a working day, so he's probably at his desk.

Sure enough, there is no answer, and I end the call disappointed and no nearer to getting any answers. I don't have Charlie's number, so I can't contact him either, so feeling like there is little else I can do, I throw my phone down onto Oli's sofa in frustration.

I briefly entertain the idea of trying to sneak out the back door and visit Damian to ask him questions face to face, but not only would that be dangerous for me to do so, but if the police find out I left my house unattended, then they'll stop bothering to provide me protection, and I really will be vulnerable then. So it seems like I'm stuck between a rock and a hard place, and bizarrely, despite being the innocent party here, I am the one feeling like I'm being kept under lock and key while the criminals are out there free to come and go from their homes as they please.

This feels backwards. All wrong. *Unfair.*

And it is.

But little did I know it, a little justice was going to be doled out that day towards the men from my past.

Damian. Charlie. The man in the balaclava.

By the time the sun had set, all three of them would be dead.

49

I kept myself busy for the rest of the afternoon by scrubbing Oli's bathroom and giving the kitchen a good clean because it looked like it had been a while since those particular rooms had enjoyed some TLC.

My brother isn't too messy, but it's clear this place has been missing a woman's touch for a while, and his standards have slipped somewhat since he lost his wife, which is understandable. But I have the place looking much more presentable now, and I even had time to alphabetise Oli's collection of books and movies, a job that wasn't exactly critical but helped me pass another half an hour without spending it all worrying about what might happen next.

By the time my brother walked through the door, his home was tidier and cleaner, not that he noticed because he looked exhausted.

'Tough day at work?' I ask him as he opens the fridge and pulls out a cold beer.

'Yeah, always the same when I've had some time off.'

I feel guilty as I watch him gulp down his lager because the only reason that he had time off was so he could look after me and make sure I was okay in the immediate aftermath of what happened at my house. But it seems the compassion he was shown by his employer when he was granted a few days off has not extended to his return to the workplace, and as he slumps down into a kitchen chair, he looks drained.

'How about I cook tonight?' I suggest, very much still eager to earn my keep and not feel like a burden around here. I'm guessing it will still be a while before the police deem it safe for me to go home and even then, I'll be reluctant to do so, so I might be getting in my brother's way for a little while longer.

But Oli doesn't answer me, and the expression on his face suggests he is mentally a million miles away.

'Chinese? Indian? Pizza?' I say, still to no response. 'Horse manure? Raw sewage?'

'Huh?'

'Oh, so you are listening to me!'

I tease my brother, and he snaps out of whatever trance he was in before we agree that we are both in the mood for pizza tonight.

I make the call to place our orders while my brother showers, and by the time he comes back downstairs, looking fresh and finally free of his day's worries, I have found us a movie to enjoy when our food arrives.

'I thought we could watch this with our pizzas,' I say, gesturing to the television with the remote control. 'It was one of our favourite films growing up, remember?'

'I do,' Oli says as he slumps down onto the sofa next to me. 'Good find. And don't think I haven't noticed all the cleaning you have done around here today. I appreciate it, sis, thank you, but you really didn't have to.'

'It's the least I can do. And I'm paying for the pizzas tonight too.'

'Wow, I could get used to this.'

'Don't get too used to it. I'll be leaving one day.'

We share a smile before a knock at the door interrupts us.

'Those pizzas were quick,' I say as I leap off the sofa. 'Can you get the door, and I'll grab the drinks from the kitchen?'

'Sure,' Oli says, and while I'm grabbing two bottles of beer from the fridge, I hear him open the front door. But I don't hear him thanking a delivery driver, nor do I smell a couple of delicious oven-cooked pizzas. I just hear several voices before sticking my head around the kitchen door, which is when I see a detective and two police officers entering the house.

'What's going on?' I ask, ditching the beers and rushing into the hallway. 'What's happened? Have you found the man in the balaclava?'

'There has been a development,' the man who introduces himself as Detective Reynolds tells me. 'Please, you and your brother, take a seat, and I'll tell you all about it.'

We do as we're told, though I'm extremely eager and impatient to find out what's happened. And then the detective begins.

'Around two o'clock this afternoon, my colleagues received a phone call from a resident at 17 Hopkins Road,' the detective says, and I immediately recognise the street name. It's where Damian lives. 'The resident was concerned about Damian, your ex-boyfriend, after he had failed to call around for lunch. Apparently, he made a habit of eating lunch with his

227

next-door neighbour every Friday when he was working from home. But he hadn't shown up that day, so the neighbour went to Damian's house to see if everything was okay. The car was in the driveway, so he figured Damian was home, but with no answer at the front door, he tried the back. It was there he found the back door kicked in, and when he went inside, he discovered Damian.'

The detective pauses for a second.

'He was dead.'

I stare at the detective while imagining my ex lifeless and alone. But I don't have to imagine too hard because I already saw a photo in which the exact thing was depicted. But this time, Damian is dead for real.

'What happened?' I ask as the photo I saw flares up in my memory.

'It appears somebody broke into his home and attacked him. We recovered a knife at the scene, and we're currently examining the weapon for fingerprints.'

'Oh my God,' I say, disbelieving. 'Why would somebody do that to him?'

'There's something else,' the detective goes on as the police officers by the window continue to stand behind Oli and me. 'A little after four o'clock this afternoon, we received another call, this time from the daughter of Charlie McGregor, your former client.'

Not Charlie as well.

'His daughter found him stabbed to death in his living room, and again, a murder weapon was found at the scene.'

I don't even have any words for the detective at the moment. This is crazy.

'When she called us to the premises, the officers quickly worked to seal off the perimeter and contain the crime scene. It was while they were doing that that they discovered another body. A male. Mid-thirties. He was at the bottom of the garden, and he, too, had been stabbed. There was blood all down the garden path leading away from the house. While it's still very early, one view is that he was the murderer, and he got injured during his attack on Charlie, trying to flee but ultimately succumbing to his own wounds before he could get away.'

My mouth is hanging wide open, and if it gets any wider, I fear my jaw might be on the floor.

'What the hell is going on?' I ask the detective. 'This doesn't make any sense.'

'We're looking into it, and we hope to have some answers soon,' the detective assures me. 'But it's possible this is connected to what happened to you, Katherine.'

'You think?' Oli cries, unable to keep his sarcasm in. 'My sister told you Damian and Charlie had something to do with this, but you didn't take it seriously.'

'We interviewed them both several times, but there was no evidence to suggest they were involved in the plot against Katherine.'

'Even though I was shown photos of them by the man in the balaclava,' I remind the detective.

'About that,' he says then, harbouring something else to add. 'It's possible that the man we found in the garden, the one who seems to have died while leaving Charlie's home, could be the man in the balaclava.'

'Really?'

I know I should stay guarded, but if there's a chance that the man who tormented me is no longer out there, then that can only be good news. It would mean I wouldn't have to look over my shoulder for the rest of my life. Things could go back to normal, or at least a new kind of normal.

'It's possible he was returning to tie up some loose ends, as it were,' Detective Reynolds says. 'But to say any more would be speculating too much, so I'll reserve judgement until we have looked into this further. But with Damian and Charlie both turning up dead on the same day, it would be a very large coincidence for there to be two separate killers.'

'This man in the garden,' Oli says. 'Do you know who he is?'

'We found identification on him, so we have a name, but we won't share that yet until we know more about his background. But officers are currently at his address, and we'll update you as soon as we know more,' Detective Reynolds says. 'I just wanted to come here and keep you abreast of the developments.'

'Yes, of course. Thank you,' I say, grateful for the update because while I'll still be worrying now, it will be a different kind of worry. I might not be in danger anymore. But what about Damian and Charlie? It's too late for them.

'What does all this mean?' I ask the detective before he can leave. 'Is it over now?'

The detective looks like he wishes he could give me the answer I want. But he's too professional, too experienced and perhaps too cynical to commit to a positive outcome for me just yet. That's why he just repeats what he said about letting me know as soon as they have any more information before he and the two officers leave my brother's house.

But I notice that the officer in the police car who has been keeping watch all day doesn't leave with them.

He's still at his post.

So that makes me think I still might be in danger.

50

Hearing the words 'we no longer feel you are in danger' from Detective Reynolds yesterday, three days after the bodies of Damian, Charlie and that other man were discovered, was a big moment for me. But returning to my house and walking through the front door is an even bigger one.

I'm home.

I beat my foes.

And I've lived to tell the tale.

'It's cold in here,' Oli says before I point him to the thermostat.

'Yeah, I guess it's been a while since the heating was on,' I say as I look around my house and wait to see if I'm bombarded with terrible flashbacks and nightmares of what happened the last time I was here. But so far, so good. I'm not envisioning Franz with his gun, nor am I seeing that man in the balaclava, the one with the knife and the one who could have so easily killed me on several occasions.

But maybe there's a simple reason why those two people are not haunting me anymore.

It's because I know they're both dead.

As the radiators around my home begin to warm up, I go up to my bedroom to unpack the few things I hurriedly threw into a bag before I went to stay at my brother's.

After tossing a few dirty items of clothing into the wash basket at the bottom of my bed and returning my toothbrush to its rightful place in the cup on my bathroom sink, I tell myself that I will give it a couple of nights here before I make a definite decision about whether or not I want to stay permanently.

I'll always have the option to sell, but I'm going to give it time and see how I feel rather than making any hasty decisions that I might live to regret. I'd hate to leave this beautiful house if I don't have to, but only time will tell if I can handle being back here where so many awful things happened.

But one thing is for sure.

If I do end up staying, I will make sure that underground cell and its connecting corridor are sealed off forever.

I can't bring myself to go back down there and see that horrible part of the house again, but I don't need to. Oli has assured me that any building works that need to be conducted to erase that part of the home's history will be sorted through him, meaning I don't have to get involved and even think about it if I don't want to.

So I won't.

I will never think about Franz, Greta and poor Karl, who surely died down there before being disposed of elsewhere by his father, ever again.

Going back downstairs, I find Oli attempting to return the favour I did for him by cleaning my house for me, but before he has finished rummaging around in the cupboard under the sink where I keep all the sanitisers, bleach bottles and dishcloths, I tell him not to bother.

'The police have done a pretty good job of cleaning this place already,' I say, looking around at my gleaming home, and I'm not wrong. They really did scrub every inch of this place once their investigation was done, or at least the cleaners they helped arrange for me did. I guess it was their way of thanking me for agreeing to move out of my home for so long while the forensics teams did their work. But I gave them all the time and space they needed, not just because my life was still under threat, but because I wanted to be absolutely sure that all of this was over before I came back here.

And it most certainly is now.

As he promised, Detective Reynolds did return when he had more news and boy, did he have some. Oli and I had listened with rapt attention and more than a little morbid curiosity as the detective had told us the fruits that his team's investigation had bore after the deaths of the three men.

After going to the address of the man who had succumbed to stab wounds in Charlie's back garden, the police discovered several things of interest, notably a bundle of cash in an envelope, printed photographs of my house and something that got everybody's attention.

A balaclava in a bedroom drawer.

The police showed me the balaclava and asked if it looked like the one my attacker wore, and while I suppose all balaclavas look the same, I knew for sure this one was the same one because the left eye hole was slightly larger than the right. Along with the other evidence, the police then believed they had the man who had held me captive and threatened my life. All they had to do then was figure out why he killed Damian and Charlie.

Because of how adamant I was that the man in the balaclava showed me a photo of Damian and Charlie appearing very much dead, Detective Reynolds worked on the theory that they must have been involved after all, and all three were working with Franz. But when the plan went awry and Franz died, the man in the balaclava fled the scene and seemed to have gotten away with it.

But knowing that I would send the police to look into Damian and Charlie and no doubt worried that they may speak to those officers and possibly give something away, like the identity of the man in the balaclava, for example, that man took it upon himself to ensure his secret remained safe. He visited each of the men and murdered them in their own homes, although things didn't go as planned with Charlie, and he garnered injuries in the attack too, injuries that proved fatal before he had time to fully leave the scene of the crime. With that, everybody involved in the plot against my life was accounted for and nullified.

And that was why I had decided to come home.

Getting a confirmation of sorts that Damian and Charlie were actually involved after all was sobering but also a stark reminder that I had to be much more careful going forward not to make any enemies out of people. I hadn't been aware that I'd been doing so, but as Detective Reynolds warned me when we spoke yesterday for the last time, there's no telling how some people will take things, so perhaps it's better in future if I don't go through life giving people short deadlines and showing little compassion for them when I do.

I know Detective Reynolds was just trying to be helpful rather than judgemental, but it was still tough to hear that I had probably brought all of this on myself. So what do I do now? Completely change how I operate? Get a new job, one that won't require me to make people do things they don't want to do? And what about how I deal with other things like house purchases, unfaithful partners and the sort? I guess I'll have to err on the side of caution and never be too aggressive or angry in my dealings just in case I rub somebody up the wrong way again.

But all of that is for another day. Tonight, I am going to enjoy being back home, and with my brother with me, I decide to suggest another takeaway. We didn't really get to enjoy our pizza last time because our heads were still swimming with the news Detective Reynolds had given us just before the delivery driver arrived. But there's nothing that can get in our way of enjoying a lovely meal tonight, and as I search in the cupboards for the takeaway menu for my local Chinese restaurant, I only have one thing on my mind - sweet and sour chicken balls.

But before I can hand the menu to Oli so he can make his selection, I hear the buzzer that tells me somebody is at the gate to my driveway.

'Who the hell could this be?' I say to Oli as I go over to the intercom, and when I look at the screen, I see Detective Reynold's face looking back at me.

My heart sinks because I thought I'd seen the last of him. Surely his appearance here can't be a good thing. What could he have to tell me now that will ruin this night?

I press the button to open the gate and let him in before going to tell Oli that we might have to put the takeaway plans on hold. My brother looks dismayed, as am I, but as the police car parks on my drive and I go to open the front door for the detective, I have no idea just how dismayed I will be in a moment's time. That's because no sooner is the door open than the detective storms in, followed quickly by four police officers, and they rush past me into the hallway.

'Your home was empty, so I figured we'd find you here,' Detective Reynolds says before the policeman behind him brandishes a pair of handcuffs. 'Oliver Wilkinson, I am arresting you on suspicion of murder.'

I watch as my brother is pushed against a wall before his wrists are cuffed. Then he is marched out of my home, right past me on the way to the door, and as he walks by, he glances at me nervously.

I expect to see a frightened look in his eyes, one not too dissimilar to the one he had back when we were kids, and he told me he had broken an ornament and wanted me to help him cover it up from our parents.

But I don't see that frightened look.

I only see the look that tells me he is not as shocked about all of this as I am.

51

'I want to hear it from him,' I tell Detective Reynolds after just being told several very disturbing things. 'I'll only believe it if it comes from his mouth.'

The detective looks a little surprised that I've made such a demand.

'We have the evidence plus his confession, albeit a reluctant one, which means he's going to go away for a very long time. You speaking to him is not going to change anything for him.'

'But it might for me,' I say. 'Please, I just want five minutes with him. I need this, and after what I've been through, it's the least you can give me.'

The detective sighs before conceding and gesturing for one of the police officers in the corridor behind him to come over. We're in the bowels of a police station with lots of uniformed officers rushing by and the occasional criminal being marched past in handcuffs before they are taken into one of the many rooms, presumably to be interviewed on tape. But my brother has already conducted his interview, and as Detective Reynolds said, the suspect was not only presented with all the evidence against him but he also confessed when it became clear he was caught.

I don't know which room my sibling is in, though, but I want to see him before he is taken to prison. Who knows, I might not have the courage to do so again, so I want to take advantage of my inner strength today and see Oli face to face one more time.

After that, I don't really care what happens to him.

'This way,' the police officer tells me after Detective Reynolds has instructed him on where to take me. I follow the officer down the corridor, passing a room with an open door in which I see what looks like an exasperated lawyer trying to convince the accused sitting next to him to stay quiet and let him do the talking.

What a job, I think to myself as I keep going. *It's one thing to be the person tasked with putting guilty people in prison but it's quite another to be the one tasked with getting guilty people out of it.*

We stop at a closed door, and the officer knocks before entering. When the door opens, I see another police officer standing in the room by the table. It's the table that my brother sits at, his head in his hands and his legs jiggling, a clear sign of nervous tension, and he doesn't look up as I walk in.

He only looks up when he hears one of the officers tell him that he has a visitor.

I don't smile at Oli when he sees me but I don't look angry either, or even disappointed. I'm emotionless, and I feel that's the only way I can be if I want to sit in the chair opposite my sibling and hear what he has to say for himself. Anything else, any expressions of anger, shock, frustration, rage or just plain pain, will not help me here. I have to hold it together long enough to let him say his piece.

But what I choose to do after that is anyone's guess.

239

The officer who showed me to the room leaves then, but the other one stays, standing behind the door after he has closed it, so I guess we're not going to have complete privacy. But I never really expected to get much privacy in a police station, so I sit down in my chair and take a deep breath. As I do, I look at the handcuffs around Oli's wrists. I guess they're the same cuffs that I saw slapped on him at my house yesterday before he was bundled into the back of a police car and driven away from my house before I could even ask him what the hell was going on.

I've since been informed about the reason for his arrest and everything that it entails, but as I told the detective, it's one thing to hear it all from someone being paid to do their job. It's quite another to hear it from not only the accused but the person who I spent many happy years growing up alongside and the person who, at one time in my life, was supposed to be the one looking out for me.

Oli can barely bring himself to make eye contact with me as he shuffles uncomfortably in his seat, and with the silence between us deafening, I guess I'll have to be the one to go first.

'You really hated me that much?' I ask him, hoping that the tears don't come now and overwhelm me before I've had the chance to have this conversation properly. 'You hated me so much that you wanted me dead?'

'I did,' Oli admits, still not looking at me.

'Because of what happened with Laura. You felt I deserved to die for that?'

240

He nods. 'She'd still be here if you hadn't made her go out that day. And we would have a son. I wouldn't be sitting here now facing the rest of my life behind bars.'

'Okay,' I say, even though it's anything but. 'If that is how you felt, then why did you come to my house that night and stop what was happening? Why did you kill Franz?'

'I changed my mind,' he says, finally meeting my eyes as if he can undo what he just said by persuading me that he decided against it in the end.

'Why?'

'It was that message you sent me earlier that day. It suddenly dawned on me what was about to happen, and I couldn't allow it. I had to try and stop it.'

'You were almost too late.'

'I know, but I did stop it. You're alive. At least I can forgive myself for that.'

Observing my brother at these close quarters, I can see that he is a shell of his former self. It looks like all the life has been drained out of him just in the twenty-four hours that he has been in police custody. The speed of the decline in his physical well-being does not bode well for all the years he has stretching ahead of him in a prison cell, but I'll reserve my sympathies until he's told me everything.

'Tell me about how it happened,' I say, aware that there is still a police officer in the room, but Oli's confession is already on tape, so anything he says now won't make much difference to what happens to him going forward. 'Tell me about how you teamed up with those other men to get revenge on me.'

'Franz came to me,' Oli says, choosing to look back down at the table between us then. 'He said he knew you, and he had read about what happened between us in the papers. Laura's accident and how we fell out after it. Remember I spoke to that journalist not long after the funeral and told him I blamed my sister for it? He read that article online. I guess that's how he knew I bore a grudge against you, just like he bore a grudge of his own too.'

'Go on.'

'He told me what happened with the house, his dream house that he never wanted to sell until his wife got sick. How you pressured him to make a decision on the sale price while he was stressed about his partner.'

'What did you say to that?'

'I said it sounded like you.'

That hurts, but I nod for Oli to tell me more.

'Franz said that he knew other people who had been mistreated by you.'

'Damian and Charlie?'

'Yeah. And another guy, though he never gave me his name.'

'The man in the balaclava?'

'Yes.'

'How did Franz find Damian and Charlie and know what happened between me and them?' I ask, trying to piece all of this together.

'He used social media to find Damian. He figured it was an ex-boyfriend of yours based on the old

242

photos, so he visited him and asked him how you guys ended.'

'Damian cheated.'

'Yes, but you threw him out and didn't forgive him, so he resented that.'

I scoff. 'And Charlie?'

'Franz stalked you online and in person. He found out where you worked and from there, he did his research, looking into company acquisitions your employers had made. That was how he found out Charlie had been involved in selling his company to you, but when Franz approached him, Charlie made it clear he had also been pressurised by you.'

'Again, I was just doing my job.'

'I'm just telling you how it happened,' Oli says, holding up his hands, although not very far apart because the handcuffs see to that. 'Whether you were justified or not doesn't matter. Franz hated you, and once he had found a few others who felt the same way, he told us he had a plan.'

'Okay, tell me about the plan.'

Oli looks strained then. 'You know what happened.'

'I want to hear it from you!'

The police officer flinches at the sound of my raised voice, and I hold up a hand by way of apology to him. Recomposing myself, I look back to my brother, who gets the message and goes on.

'Franz had each of us playing a role. Damian and Charlie just had to pose for the photos, so it looked like they were dead. That would be used to scare you and get you to take what was happening seriously.'

'As if all the other things wouldn't,' I say, disgusted.

'The man in the balaclava would start things on the night by posting the letter, then we were going to see what you did. But in case you ran, he covered the back of the house, and Greta had the front. You went to the back, so he got you and took you back in. From there, he was only supposed to show you the timer, show you the photos of Damian and Charlie and get you thinking about the past and the things you'd done. He was to keep you tied up until Franz got there. But you escaped and went to your neighbours, which complicated things.'

'Wait, before all of that, I put my phone in a drawer upstairs, but it was missing when I went to look for it. How did that happen?'

'Franz was hiding in your house the whole time,' Oli tells me, speaking like it's no big deal and not the terrifying statement that it actually is.

'He was in my house before I even got home that night?'

Oli nods. 'He designed the house, right? Well, that underground corridor and cell had another way into it. There's a hatch in the garden, though no one would ever know it to look at it as it just looks like part of the path. He went in there and got under the house, then he sneaked out and hid upstairs once you had turned off the house alarm. He moved your phone and then hid again.'

'You've got to be kidding me.'

'He told me he designed that underground space for security reasons.'

'Security? How the hell is that security?'

'It gave him and his family a way to escape the home if they ever felt threatened.'

'Do you know what else he used it for besides terrorising me? He locked his son down there and most likely killed him.'

'I don't know anything about that. He never mentioned his son.'

Now it's my turn to hold my head in my hands.

'So what was your part in all of this?' I ask after I've had a few moments to calm down.

'I was supposed to come with Franz. He figured it would be even more shocking for you if I walked in alongside him. But I didn't meet him when I was supposed to. I'd changed my mind about going along with the plan.'

'I almost died.'

'But I got there in time. I surprised Franz when I did show up and was able to get the gun from him. I shot him and wanted to kill the guy in the balaclava too, but you stopped me going after him, so he got away.'

'I stopped you because I thought you were on my side!'

'I was! At that point, anyway. But because that man got away, I knew it was a problem because none of us knew who he actually was. Only Franz knew, and he was dead. The rest of us had never seen his face. We figured he was just some guy who Franz had hired to carry out the violent parts of the plan so that we didn't have to.'

All that covers what happened before that night and the events of the night itself. But there's still so much more, and that's what I want to know about now.

'Tell me about how you got caught,' I say, and Oli shakes his head then.

'I was stupid. I should have just left things. But I was so worried about that man in the balaclava. Who he was. What he was capable of. And what he might do to me after I had ruined the plan and killed Franz.'

'So what happened?'

'The only thing I had for him was a number. There was a group that Franz had set up in which we sent messages before that night. So I contacted the man in the balaclava individually and told him I was sorry.'

'For spoiling things?'

'Yeah, that and for shooting at him. It was a safe assumption that he hated me and probably wanted me dead in return. And I was right. He messaged me and said that I was a dead man, not just for shooting at him but because the police were now on our case, and we might all end up getting caught.'

Oli's face is so pale, but I imagine it was even paler when he received that message calling him a dead man.

'So what did you do?'

'Well, I panicked obviously because how can I defend myself against a man who wants me dead if I don't even know who he is? And I could hardly go to the police about it either, could I?'

246

'I guess not.'

'But then I had an idea. I came up with a plan, a way that the both of us could get away with it so that he wouldn't have to worry about the police. I said we should kill Damian and Charlie and then have a third body, somebody who we could pass off as the man in the balaclava. That way, the police would figure that everybody involved was dead, and the case would be closed.'

'And he went for it?'

'Yeah. He said it might work and if it did, then we would be even. But I had to be the one who did the killing, not him.'

'Oh my God.'

I'm physically shaking because even though I already heard all this from Detective Reynolds earlier today, it's different hearing it coming from my brother.

My brother, the murderer.

'You know, I thought you killing Franz was okay because you were trying to save me,' I say. 'But killing Damian and Charlie and whoever that other guy was. That was in cold blood. That's something different. It's so much worse.'

'I know! Do you think I would have done it if there was any other way out of this for me? I had no choice. That man was going to come back and kill me unless I did this. And he might have come back for you too.'

'Don't pretend like you killed those people for me!' I cry, disgusted to be used as a motive for all the crimes. The officer flinches again, but I don't apologise

247

this time, nor do I lower the volume of my voice as I get up from my seat and point a finger at my brother.

'You did not have to kill them! And you're only sorry because you got caught!'

I believe all of that to be true but especially the last part. Oli thought he could get away with all of this, but he had no idea that there were cameras at Charlie's home, small ones, imperceptible to the eye of those who didn't know where to look, but they were there and because they were, they captured Oli killing Charlie as well as dragging the body of the dead man into the garden.

'Who was that other guy?' I ask my brother. 'How did you choose him?'

'The man in the balaclava gave me his profile. Height. Build. Hair and eye colour. I just had to find someone who fit the profile.'

'For me to identify?'

Oli nods.

'That man was innocent. He might have been a father!'

'No, I checked and made sure he wasn't.'

'Oh, you checked before you stabbed him to death and framed him for several crimes by planting evidence at his place? How wonderfully considerate of you!'

'I think that's enough,' the police officer says, stepping towards the table.

'Yes, I think it is, too,' I say, snarling at my brother. But before I leave, I have one more thing to say to him, and I keep it in mind even as he tries apologising to me one more time.

'Laura would be ashamed of you,' I tell him before walking out of the room, and as I go down the corridor, I think about how I once thought I would never see my brother again.

But this time, I know it's for real.

52

It's been six months since I talked to my brother at the police station, just before he was hauled away to a cell where he remains to this day, waiting for his official hearing and sentencing. But I've been keeping myself busy in that time, trying not to dwell on the past and choosing to look ahead to the future instead.

It's a future that will be taking place in very different surroundings.

The reason for me being so busy is because I decided that I was going to sell my house and move on to fresh pastures. Therefore, I've spent the last half a year dealing with estate agents, both for the property I'm selling and the one I'm moving into. I viewed plenty of places before settling on a new home that felt right for me, and I've opted for a medium-sized townhouse, one that was built back in the sixties rather than in the last decade by a crazy German man who constructed secret cells, corridors and doors under it. But it was much easier for me to find a new house than it was to find somebody willing to buy my old one.

While the property itself looks fantastic on the face of it, I wasn't helped by the fact that the media had reported so extensively on the horrors that happened in it, meaning everybody in this town knew the history of the house and why I was ultimately selling. Dead bodies, secret underground rooms and the brother of the homeowner being guilty of killing multiple people does not make for a quick sale, although it did ensure that several of the people who came to view the place were merely there out of morbid curiosity.

I had to chase one man out of my dining room when he kept taking photos before asking me exactly which chair it was that I had been tied to. Rather than explain to him that the chair had been broken during my ordeal, I just kicked him out before calling my estate agent and telling him that from now on, only virtual viewings were allowed.

But after spending a while fearing that I'd never be able to get rid of this place and truly move on with my life, despite reducing the asking price several times, an offer came in that I was only too glad to accept. I don't know too much about the person or persons moving in, only that I made sure I was pleasant in all dealings with them whenever my estate agent asked me to do anything to move the sale along so that they can't feel aggrieved and decide to take revenge on me in the years to come.

It seems silly but I honestly have to be careful with everything I do now because one thing this whole experience has taught me is that people do not forget when they feel they have been slighted somehow.

With the sale completed, I went to work packing all my belongings into boxes, and it is those boxes that are now being carried from my house and placed into the back of two big removals vans by the men I am paying to help me move. Minute by minute, this place is getting emptier, and it won't be long until there is nothing left but bare rooms, the walls and floors completely free for somebody else to come in and make their mark on.

Every house has a history, but thankfully, these walls can't talk, so they can't tell the new owners every sordid detail about what went on here. Well, not unless Franz installed some hi-tech equipment there too, and to be honest, I wouldn't put anything past that man anymore.

I step outside the house to watch the last of my boxes get put into the vans, and I'm grateful that it's a lovely summer's morning with barely a cloud in the sky. Soaking up a little sun as I stand on my driveway and prepare to kiss goodbye to this address once and for all, I see the roof of my neighbour's house peeking above the hedges to my right and when I do, I think of the people who live there.

Norma and Fred, the couple I barely knew until I suddenly found myself running to their home in a desperate bid to survive. But if I didn't know much about them before, I sure know a lot about them now.

Norma is back on her feet and fully recovered from the fall she suffered earlier in the year, although with no thanks to the nurse who was supposed to be bringing her back to health. I didn't forget about what I saw Rosie do that night with the pillow and that was why, after the dust had settled a little bit after Oli's arrest, I went to see her in her workplace at the hospital.

It was there that I used the fact that my own brother was in prison for murder to threaten her with an act of violence herself. I told her that she had to quit being a nurse as soon as possible, or I would report what I saw to the police. Not only that, but I had Fred back on my side, and he was willing to report that he was pressured into helping her if it came to that. And the cherry on top was if she refused to do what I asked, I would hurt her, not there but one day, when she was going about her business, and why wouldn't I?

Violence ran in my family, after all.

Rosie did as I asked and quit her nursing role immediately, removing herself from her position so that she wouldn't have access to any vulnerable people again. But I will make sure to keep tabs on her, just to ensure she is still on the straight and narrow, as it were.

As for Fred, I have allowed him to enjoy the rest of his retirement beside his wife, confident that he was talked into doing something heinous by Rosie, just like Greta was by Franz. But I'll keep tabs on him too. It's not as if I don't know where he lives.

But after what he and Rosie went through with that man in the balaclava, they have learnt to fear me because while they were tied up in a bedroom, I'm the woman who beat that intruder, and that is a fact that makes me seem a whole lot scarier than I actually am.

As I look away from the top of Fred and Norma's house, I see my postman making his way through the myriad of removals men on the driveway, and when he reaches me, he has a letter for me.

'Thank you,' I say as I take it before telling him something he may or may not be interested in. 'I've had all my important mail redirected, but I suppose there are always a few things that slip through. Hopefully, the new owners will pass anything on if it comes.'

The postman smiles at me before heading away, almost tripping over a stray box of my kitchen pans as he goes before I turn my attention to the letter in my hand. Despite knowing that it's silly, there is still a small part of me that gets anxious every time I have some new post to open.

It's hard not to remember the letter that came through my door that Friday night that told me I only had an hour to live, even if I have massively outlived that deadline.

Opening the letter, I tell myself that it won't be anything as harrowing as that and sure enough, it isn't. Just a notice from the local church about a fundraising event happening on the last Sunday of the month. I won't be around for that because I'm moving to the other side of town, but then I consider making the effort and coming back for it if only to see if they need an extra pair of hands helping out on any of the stalls.

Nearly everything that came out of my ordeal was negative, but one good thing is that I feel I am more compassionate and aware of helping others. I guess I was guilty of being too selfish in the past, only placing importance on my needs rather than taking into account anybody else's. But I am striving to be better in that area now, as I perhaps should have done years ago.

Folding the letter and stuffing it into the back pocket of my jeans, I give a thumbs up to the removal man, who tells me that every box is packed, and the house is now empty. As he goes to get in one of the trucks alongside his colleagues, I take the house keys from my pocket before approaching the front door.

There is a small temptation to go back inside and have one last walk around the place I once called home, but I decide not to give in to it, opting to close the front door and lock it quickly instead because I'm committed to going forward, not back. Now all I have to do is drive to the estate agent's office and drop the keys off, and then I'll be rid of this place for good, so that's what I'll do now, hopping in behind the wheel of my car, the one that has new tyres after the previous ones were slashed.

I wait for the removal vans to reverse off my driveway before I do the same, and once I'm on the main road, I hit the button on my key fob that closes the main gates. Catching one final glimpse of my house before the gate seals shut, I feel very little emotion and realise this is easier than I thought it would be. Then again, why should leaving behind a bad place be difficult?

Good riddance to this house.

And good riddance to all those who thought they could kill me in it.

But as is life, it's never quite as simple as that, and I've barely made it to the end of the main road before I remember the one thing that means I'll never get full closure on what happened that fateful Friday night six months ago.

It's knowing that the man in the balaclava was never identified and caught.

As Detective Reynolds has told me several times, no doubt to try and reassure me, whoever that man behind the mask was, he would be a fool to come back to try and hurt me now because as long as he stays away, then he is a free man. He can only get caught by making a mistake, and if he has any brains about him, then he won't risk making one. The detective also reminded me that the man in the balaclava was most likely being paid by Franz to carry out a job for him, and now Franz is dead, there's no incentive for that man to come back if he's not getting anything for it.

I guess that all makes sense and is true.

Or at least I have to hope it is anyway.

But as an added layer of security, it was recommended to me that I change address, as well as workplace, so anybody out there who might still want to hurt me would have a harder time tracking me down. That made my decision to sell up and move even easier, and I have done just that, as well as handing in my resignation at work, something I perhaps should have done a long time ago. That job was not healthy and made me do things I regret, but I'll make sure my next one is something I can be prouder of.

Turning off my old street and pressing down on the accelerator so that I can get to the estate agent's office quicker, my hands grip the steering wheel, the same hands that once had to fight to keep me alive. But I'm still here, and while the man in the balaclava might still be out there somewhere too, I refuse to be the one who spends the rest of my life looking over my shoulder.

He's the criminal, not me.

So he can do the worrying.

Meanwhile, I'll get busy doing the living, and I'll start as soon as I get the keys to my new home.

EPILOGUE

The van that followed Katherine's car from her old house towards her new one was full of all sorts of things. Letters, parcels, and one slightly more unusual item, which was kept in the glove compartment, hidden out of view so nobody else would see it.

Only the driver needed to know it was there, and he would take it out but not yet. He'd wait for the right moment, one that would surely present itself soon enough, once the woman he was following was in her new house and feeling like she was safe again.

The item in question was a balaclava, and the man driving the van was thankful for it because it had been another one just like it that had been the only thing that had kept Katherine or anybody else from identifying him and therefore, the only thing that had kept him out of prison.

While the plan to kill Katherine had not gone to plan, it did amuse the man who had got away with it that he was still able to get so close to the woman without her knowing who he really was. As far as Katherine was concerned, he was just her postman, or rather her old postman now she was moving house, and it had stayed that way right up until today when he had just handed her a letter outside the home she had sold.

Katherine didn't suspect a thing. She just took the letter and let the postman walk away, and why wouldn't she?

If only she knew he was the man who had held a knife to her throat and taken her to hell and back.

Having been her postman for well over a year, the man driving the van was only a small, practically insignificant part of Katherine's life. But while she had never paid much attention to him, he had always paid attention to her.

Like the time he had been trying to put a letter in the post box outside her front gate, and she had almost hit him with her car as she was reversing off the driveway. She hit the brakes at the last second, but did she apologise? No, she just looked incredulously at the postman as if it was his fault she hadn't been looking where she was going before she sped away.

Or like the time he had a big parcel to drop off, so he used the buzzer to see if she would open the gate so he could deliver it to the door because it wouldn't fit in the post box. He heard Katherine huffing through the intercom before she eventually agreed to open the gates but not before she told him to make sure he stayed away from the grass and the flowerbeds, something he had always been careful to do, which made her concerns unwarranted, if not downright disrespectful.

And who could forget the time when something Katherine had sent in the post had failed to reach its intended destination, and she decided to shout at him about it, despite it not being his fault at all. But that didn't matter to Katherine, who said all sorts of rude things before she sped away in her fancy car once again.

That was usually how it went with Katherine. She barely spoke to her postman but when she did, it was usually to discipline him about something. But that was a mistake. After all, it was the postman who was the one who had been on very friendly terms with Franz, the previous homeowner he used to deliver mail to, so much so that he even had the email address for the man who moved to Germany. That was how they corresponded when Franz was overseas, and that was how the postman learnt about Katherine being rude to the homeowner too.

And that was when the postman came up with the plan to get back at Katherine.

The postman was the man in the balaclava, and pretty soon, he would be donning another balaclava again to pay Katherine another visit.

But this time, there would be no timer.

An hour had been too generous for her.

Next time, it would be quick.

There was no doubt that the woman driving the car that he was following had learnt some lessons after what had happened to her. She had learnt to treat certain people better, like those she sold her house to, those she did business with and even those she called family. But there was someone else who she should have been more careful about in the past.

The postman.

She should never have forgotten to be nice to the man who came to her house every day and knew her routine.

Who knew when she went out and when she came home.

And, of course, who knew how to push a note through her letterbox to put the whole plan in motion.

THE END

Download My Free Book

If you would like to receive a FREE copy of my psychological thriller 'Just One Second', then you can find the link to the book at my website www.danielhurstbooks.com

Thank you for reading *Her Last Hour*. My aim with this one was to keep you on the edge of your seat and guessing at the end of every chapter. I hope you enjoyed it!

If you have enjoyed this psychological thriller, then you'll be pleased to know that I have several more stories in this genre, and you can find a list of my titles on the next page. These include my most popular book *Til Death Do Us Part*, which has a twist that very few people have been able to predict, and *The Doctor's Wife*, which became the #1 selling book in the UK Kindle Store in February 2023.

ALSO BY DANIEL HURST

TIL DEATH DO US PART

What if your husband was your worst enemy?

Megan thinks that she has the perfect husband and the perfect life. Craig works all day so that she doesn't have to, leaving her free to relax in their beautiful and secluded country home. But when she starts to long for friends and purpose again, Megan applies for a job in London, much to her husband's disappointment. She thinks he is upset because she is unhappy. But she has no idea.

When Megan secretly attends an interview and meets a recruiter for a drink, Craig decides it is time to act. Locking her away in their home, Megan realises that her husband never had her best interests at heart. Worse, they didn't meet by accident. Craig has been planning it all from the start.

As Megan is kept shut away from the world with only somebody else's diary for company, she starts to uncover the lies, the secrets, and the fact that she isn't actually Craig's first wife after all...

THE PASSENGER

She takes the same train every day. But this is a journey she will never forget...

Amanda is a hardworking single mum, focused on her job and her daughter, Louise. But it's also time she did something for herself, and after saving for years, she is now close to quitting her dreary 9-5 and following her dream.

But then, on her usual commute home from London to Brighton, she meets a charming stranger – a man who seems to know everything about her. Then he delivers an ultimatum. She needs to give him the code to her safe where she keeps her savings before they reach Brighton – or she will never see Louise again.

Amanda is horrified, but while she knows the threat is real, she can't give him the code. That's because the safe contains something other than her money. It holds a secret. *A secret so terrible it will destroy both her's and her daughter's life if it ever gets out...*

THE WRONG WOMAN

What if you were the perfect person to get revenge?

Simone used to be the woman other women would use if they suspected their partner was cheating. She would investigate, find out the truth and if the men were guilty, exact revenge in one form or another. But after things went wrong with one particular couple, Simone was forced to go into hiding to evade the law.

Having assumed a new identity, Simone is now Mary, a mild-mannered woman who doesn't raise her voice or get angry, meaning nobody would ever suspect her of being capable of the things she used to do for a living. But when she finds out that her new boyfriend is having an affair, it awakens in her the person she used to be. Plotting revenge, Mary reverts back to the woman she once was before she went on the run and became domesticated. That means Simone is back, and it also means that her boyfriend and his mistress are in for the shock of their lives.

They messed with her. *But they picked the wrong woman.*

THE WOMAN AT THE DOOR

It was a perfect Saturday night. *Until she knocked on the door...*

Rebecca and Sam are happily married and enjoying a typical Saturday night until a knock at the door changes everything. There's a woman outside, and she has something to say. Something that will change the happy couple's relationship forever...

With their marriage thrown into turmoil, Rebecca no longer knows who to trust, while Sam is determined to find out who that woman was and why she came to their house. But the problem is that he doesn't know who she is and why she has targeted them.

Desperate to save his marriage, Sam is willing to do anything to find the truth, even if it means breaking the law. But as time goes by and things only seem to get worse, it looks like he could lose Rebecca forever.

THE NEIGHBOURS

It seemed like the perfect house on the perfect street. *Until they met the neighbours...*

Happily married couple, Katie and Sean, have plenty to look forward to as they move into their new home and plan for the future. But then they meet two of their new neighbours, and everything on their quiet street suddenly doesn't seem as desirable as it did before.

Having been warned about the other neighbours and their adulterous and criminal ways, Katie and Sean realise that they are going to have to be on their guard if they want to make their time here a happy one.

But some of the other neighbours seem so nice, and that's why they choose to ignore the warning and get friendly with the rest of the people on the street. *And that is why their marriage will never be the same again...*

THE TUTOR

What if you invited danger into your home?

Amy is a loving wife and mother to her husband, Nick, and her two children, Michael and Bella. It's that dedication to her family that causes her to seek help for her teenage son when it becomes apparent that he is going to fail his end of school exams.

Enlisting the help of a professional tutor, Amy is certain that she is doing the best thing for her son and, indeed, her family. But when she discovers that there is more to this tutor than meets the eye, it is already too late.

With the rest of her family enamoured by the tutor, Amy is the only one who can see that there is something not quite right about her. But as the tutor becomes more involved in Amy's family, it's not just the present that is threatened. Secrets from the past are exposed too, and by the time everything is out in the open, Amy isn't just worried about her son and his exams anymore. She is worried for the survival of her entire family.

HE WAS A LIAR

What if you never really knew the man you loved?

Sarah is in a loving relationship with Paul, a seemingly perfect man who she is hoping to marry and start a family with one day, until his sudden death sends her into a world of pain.

Trying to come to terms with her loss, Sarah finds comfort in going through some of Paul's old things, including his laptop and his emails. But after finding something troubling, Sarah begins to learn things about Paul that she never knew before, and it turns out he wasn't as perfect as she thought. But as she unravels more about his secretive past, she ends up not only learning things that break her heart, but things that the police will be interested to know too.

Sarah can't believe what she has discovered. But it's only when she keeps digging that she realises it's not just her late boyfriend's secrets that are contained on the laptop. Other people's secrets are too, and they aren't dead, which means they will do anything to protect them.

RUN AWAY WITH ME

What if your partner was wanted by the police?

Laura is feeling content with her life. She is married, she has a good home, and she is due to give birth to her first child any day now. But her perfect world is shattered when her husband comes home flustered and afraid. He's made a terrible mistake. He's done a bad thing. *And now the police are going to be looking for him.*

There's only one way out of this. He wants to run. *But he won't go without his wife...*

Laura knows it is wrong. She knows they should stay and face the music. But she doesn't want to lose her man. She can't raise this baby alone. *So she agrees to go with him.* But life on the run is stressful and unpredictable, and as time goes by, Laura worries she has made a terrible mistake. They should never have ran. But it's too late for that now. Her life is ruined. The only question is: *how will it end?*

THE ROLE MODEL

She raised her. Now she must help her...

Heather is a single mum who has always done what's best for her daughter, Chloe. From childhood up to the age of seventeen, Chloe has been no trouble. That is until one night when she calls her mother with some shocking news. There's been an accident. *And now there's a dead body...*

As always, Heather puts her daughter's safety before all else, but this might be one time when she goes too far. Instead of calling the emergency services, Heather hides the body, saving her daughter from police interviews and public outcry.

But as she well knows, everything she does has an impact on her child's behaviour, and as time goes on and the pair struggle to keep their sordid secret hidden, Heather begins to think that she hasn't been such a good mum after all. *In fact, she might have been the worst role model ever...*

THE BROKEN VOWS

He broke his word to her. Now she wants revenge…

Alison is happily married to Graham, or at least she is until she finds out that he has been cheating on her. Graham has broken the vows he made on his wedding day. How could he do it? It takes Alison a while to figure it out, but at least she has time on her side. *Only that is where she is wrong.*

A devastating diagnosis means the clock is ticking down on her life now, and if she wants revenge on her cheating partner, then she is going to have to act fast. Alison does just that, implementing a dangerous and deadly plan, and it's one that will have far reaching consequences for several people, including her clueless husband.

WE USED TO LIVE HERE

How much do you know about your house?

When the Burgess family move into their 'forever'
home, it seems like they are set for many happy years
together at their new address. Steph and Grant, along
with their two children, Charlie and Amelia, settle into
their new surroundings quickly. But then they receive a
visit from a couple who claim to have lived in their
house before and wish to have a look around for old
time's sake. They seem pleasant and plausible, so Steph
invites them in. And that's when things start to change…

It's not long after the peculiar visit when the
homeowners start to find evidence of the past all around
their new home as they redecorate. But it's the discovery
of a hidden wall containing several troubling messages
that really sends Steph into a spin, and after digging
deeper into the history of the house a little more, she
learns it is connected to a shocking crime from the past.
A crime that still remains unsolved…

***Every house has secrets. But some don't stay buried
forever…***

THE 20 MINUTES SERIES

THE 20 MINUTES SERIES (in order)

20 MINUTES ON THE TUBE
20 MINUTES LATER
20 MINUTES IN THE PARK
20 MINUTES ON HOLIDAY
20 MINUTES BY THE THAMES
20 MINUTES AT HALLOWEEN
20 MINUTES AROUND THE BONFIRE
20 MINUTES BEFORE CHRISTMAS
20 MINUTES OF VALENTINE'S DAY
20 MINUTES TO CHANGE A LIFE
20 MINUTES IN LAS VEGAS
20 MINUTES IN THE DESERT

20 MINUTES ON THE ROAD
20 MINUTES BEFORE THE WEDDING
20 MINUTES IN COURT
20 MINUTES BEHIND BARS
20 MINUTES TO MIDNIGHT
20 MINUTES BEFORE TAKE OFF
20 MINUTES IN THE AIR
20 MINUTES UNTIL IT'S OVER

About The Author

Daniel Hurst lives in the Northwest of England with his wife, Harriet, and considers himself extremely fortunate to be able to write stories every day for his readers.

You can visit him at his online home
www.danielhurstbooks.com

You can connect with Daniel on Facebook at
www.facebook.com/danielhurstbooks or on Instagram at
www.instagram.com/danielhurstbooks

He is always happy to receive emails from readers at
daniel@danielhurstbooks.com and replies to every single
one.

Thank you for reading.

Daniel

Made in the USA
Las Vegas, NV
14 October 2023

79098679R00163